TALON JUSTICE

TALON
BOOK 2

BRENT TOWNS

ROUGH
EDGES
PRESS

Talon Justice
Paperback Edition
Copyright © 2022 Brent Towns

Rough Edges Press
An Imprint of Wolfpack Publishing
9850 S. Maryland Parkway, Suite A-5 #323
Las Vegas, Nevada 89183

roughedgespress.com

Paperback ISBN 978-1-68549-189-5
eBook ISBN 978-1-68549-188-8
LCCN 2022948187

TALON JUSTICE

PREVIOUSLY...

THE LOCKS on the steel door opened and the heavy metal structure swung back with a squeal of protest. Anja Meyer walked in through the opening and sat down opposite Leonid Fedorov, a stainless-steel table separating them. Leonid smiled and raised his chained hands. "Maybe?"

Anja gave him a tired smile. "Not in this lifetime."

The Russian shrugged. "It was worth a try."

"Your intelligence worked out. We took Rossi off the board and his brothels have all been shut down. We were able to cross off twenty women who were trafficked to his establishments."

"Is that all?" Leonid asked nonchalantly. Then he smiled. "I figured it would be at least double that. I suppose some is better than none at all. How are your wounds? You look to have recovered rather well."

Anja's left hand streaked across the table, grabbing the chains attached to his wrists and tugging them forward. As Leonid lurched partially across the table Anja's right hand, palm out, smashed into the center of his face, flattening his nose. "You're a despicable human being," she hissed as blood splattered from the broken snout.

Leonid reeled back, blood streaming, tears rolling down his cheeks. "You bitch," he screeched. "You fucking bitch."

Anja stood up. "Have fun rotting in prison for the next two hundred years, asshole."

"Wait," Leonid shouted after her.

Anja took another step before turning back. "What?"

"Hakim Anwar."

She stared at him, her hands on her hips in expectation. "What about him?"

"I can help you get him." His mashed face held a pleading look as he stared up at her.

"How?"

"He bought some girls from Medusa. They were transported to Sudan."

"What for?"

"There is a terrorist training camp in the Nubian desert. They are short of women."

Anja felt her heart lurch. She moved back across to the chair and sat down and took out her cell. She opened the recording app and said, "Tell me all you know."

CHAPTER ONE

"I NEED HIM ALIVE, Jake, remember that." Anja Meyer told Hawk in no uncertain terms. "He's the only one who can give us the exact location of the camp in Sudan."

Jacob Hawk, Talon's lead field agent trod forcefully on the brakes of the Mercedes-Benz E-Class Coupe, swung hard right, and stomped on the gas, making the rear end slide outward on the damp, orange lamplit cobblestone street. "I'll do my best."

"And when you get back, we'll talk about you stealing expensive vehicles."

He pictured her eyebrows pinched together beneath the short blonde hair of her bangs in a frown as she paced back and forth on slim legs which matched her athletic frame. Her mind was sharp, a trademark of her time as a team leader for the German Intelligence Services. She gave her best and expected nothing less from her people in return.

Hawk worked the brakes, clutch, gears, and wheel simultaneously as he took the next left. The hard muscles

3

of his solid frame rippled beneath his shirt as they fought hard to get the vehicle around the tight corner.

Brown eyes danced left and right, taking in the former SAS man's darkened surroundings as they slipped by the exterior of the Mercedes. He felt sweat from his exertions trickle from his brow just below his dark hair down the side of his unshaven face. He was thirty, four years younger than his boss, and at six-four, he was a man who could take care of himself.

"Where the hell is he?" Hawk snapped. "I've lost him."

The next voice he heard was that of Ilse Geller. She was Talon's intel officer and worked closely with Hawk when planning operations such as the one he was on at the moment. "He's running parallel to you, one block over, Jake," she said. "He looks to be shaping—yes, he's just turned right and is heading away from you as we speak."

"Shit," Hawk hissed.

"Jake, you'll need to take—crap, that'll do it."

Hawk had turned right at the first street he came to. The tires chirped on the pavement as the Mercedes made the turn. His eyes widened as he floored the gas pedal and saw the truck coming at him and was forced to swerve up onto the sidewalk to avoid it.

"Be aware, Jake," Ilse said calmly, "that is a one-way street."

"No shit," he growled and felt the jolt as the vehicle came off the sidewalk and back onto the road. Just as well it was dark or there would have been— "Whoa!" He swung violently on the wheel to avoid a pedestrian crossing the street.

"You need to be careful, Jake," Ilse said to him.

"Do you want this asshole or not?" Hawk growled.

"Tone, Jake," Anja cautioned him.

"Tone my frigging ass," he growled.

"I heard that."

"You were meant to."

"Jake, watch the—" Ilse stopped, watching her screen in the ops room.

Hawk's Mercedes blew out of the side street through an intersection barely missing an Audi crossing it at the same time. "That was close," he snapped. "You could have warned me about it."

"You're doing seventy, Jake. By the time I see them you're bloody past them," Ilse shot back at him. "Just drive. Make a left at the next intersection."

"Which one?"

"The one you just blew through doing eighty. Damn it, Jake. Take the next one."

The tires locked on the damp street and the Mercedes drifted around the corner when he hit the gas once more. Orange streetlamps continued to flash past and up ahead he saw traffic lights— "Shit!"

The lights changed to red around five car lengths before he reached them. A black SUV pulled away from the lights and out into the middle of the intersection just as he arrived. "Talk to me, Jake," Anja said, unable to see what Ilse was.

The intel officer closed her eyes as she waited for the explosion of metal and debris.

WHAM!

His driver's side mirror was smashed off as it clipped the rear corner of the SUV as Hawk tried to evade the threatened carnage. The rear of the Mercedes wobbled before it straightened out. "That was fun," he said in a low voice.

"Are you alright?"

"If I was any better, I'd be dangerous."

"That's what I was afraid of," Anja muttered.

"Jake, can you hear me?"

"Karl! My OCD friend, been cleaning your seat

5

where I spilled chocolate on it?" Hawk grinned, picturing Karl's frown.

"What?"

"Knock it off, Jake," Ilse said.

Karl was a recent addition to the team after the unfortunate demise of one of their members. Karl had been part of a group serving in Berlin with Anja along with Ilse. He was a former field agent who had been captured and tortured resulting in his OCD. "Sorry, Karl, what is it?"

"It doesn't matter, Jake," he said in a calm voice. "Just watch that wall coming at you."

"Fuck!" Hawk exclaimed as he went for his brakes, the large brick facade of the building in front of the Mercedes growing rapidly larger through his windshield.

The front bumper stopped half an inch from the obstruction and Hawk heard Karl chuckle. "Great driving, Jake, but your target is getting away."

"Cor, Blimey. The last thing to go through my mind was almost my ass on that one."

"If you all are finished frigging around," Anja growled, "there is a target to catch."

Hawk found reverse and the wheels spun as it shot backward. Then again as he picked out a forward gear and reefed the wheel to the right, the rear of the vehicle kicking around. "Talk to me, people."

"Take the next right, Jake," Ilse said. "You'll need to floor it because he's getting away."

Jake came to the turn, dropped back a couple of gears, and then gave the machine everything it had. As the speedometer climbed past one-hundred, Karl's voice came over the comms. "It seems that your little midnight performance has attracted the attention of the local authorities, Jake. I just intercepted an emergency radio call diverting all possible police vehicles into the area along with a helicopter."

"Where is this tosser headed?"

"Left turn then right, Jake," Ilse said.

"I'm not sure what his destination is, Jake," Anja said. "Just don't lose him."

Hawk made the next turns and was closing on another intersection when he saw the blue and red lights strobing off a building at a fast-approaching intersection.

"Jake—" Ilse started.

"I see them."

Instead of slowing, Hawk went faster, trying to beat the police car through the intersection.

He almost made it.

Almost.

"Bollocks!"

He braked hard, swung on the wheel, and lost all control as the Mercedes started a slow, skidding spin. "Hang on, Jake, this is going to hurt."

Three Hours Earlier...

"The target's name is Dedrick Erkens," Anja told Jake as they stood around the desk in the mobile ops room. A picture of him was passed from Anja to Hawk, who then handed it on to Ilse.

"What did he do?"

"He has ties to Hakim Anwar," Anja replied. "He's like a shipping contractor. Leonid informs me that he was the one responsible for shipping a handful of young women to the Nubian desert where there is a terrorist training camp. He is the only one, apart from Anwar, who knows where the camp is. We need him alive."

Leonid Federov had once been high up in Medusa, the worldwide sex trafficking corporation.

Anja's eyes focused on Hawk. There was a disappointed expression on his face. "I'm sorry, Jake, I know you hoped when I mentioned Belgium that we were going after Lars Akker. This is actionable intelligence we have, and it needs acting upon."

Hawk nodded. "It's all right, ma'am."

"We'll get him, Jake," Ilse said.

He looked at her. She was around his age with mousy brown hair and fine features. She had come to Talon with Anja and as their intelligence officer she stood out. Plus, she was more than capable in the field as well.

"I get it. We take him and we're one step closer to closing Medusa down and taking Medvedev off the board."

"Exactly," Anja acknowledged. "Speaking of Medusa for the moment, these arrived earlier from MI6."

A small bag was placed on the desk. She emptied the contents onto the polished surface, and they stood looking down at three long cylindrical items, not unlike a ballpoint pen. She picked one up and held it for everyone to see. "This is what the technical boffins are calling a mini-wand. You turn it on, and it neutralizes the tracking isotope that Medusa uses in their tattoos. You just have to wave it slowly over the affected area and it does the rest."

"How does that work?" Hawk asked.

Anja gave it to the former SAS man and said, "I have no idea. Just don't lose it."

Hawk held it up in front of his eyes and frowned. "It doesn't look like much."

"Just as long as it works. Now, back to the mission."

"Where do I come in?" Hawk asked.

"There is a nightclub in central Antwerp—"

"There always is," Hawk said skeptically.

Anja glared at him.

"Sorry."

"Intel says that the target runs the nightclub for Hakim Anwar, the actual man we're after."

"Then why not go after him?" Jake asked.

"Because I want those girls before they're lost to the rest of the world."

"They could well be already," Hawk pointed out.

Anja's eyes grew flinty. "No. I won't accept that until I see it myself. Until then, they are prisoners who need rescuing. Erkens gives us that opportunity."

"All right, keep going."

"Erkens will be at a restaurant for dinner tonight—"

"Not at the club?"

"No. He's meeting with a banker. According to Leonid, the banker's name is Daan Evers. He does all of Anwar's banking in Europe."

"Do we pick him up, too?" Hawk asked.

"No. We mark him and leave him out there until we need him. If we need him."

"Do we have Grizz and the boys on this one?"

"No. Just you. I'm sure you are quite capable of handling it."

Hawk grinned. "That's what I like, a woman with confidence."

"And if you can't I'll just fire you."

Ilse grinned at him.

———

Present Time...

In some uncanny deal of fate, the Mercedes spun in a straight line along the street. Hawk opened his eyes as it stopped and said, "Fucking bollocks. You don't see that every day."

The flashing police lights brought him back to the urgent issue at hand. The officers had stopped and were approaching his stolen vehicle. Each had a weapon raised and were shouting at him. "Get out of the car! Get out of the car!"

"Jake, you need to do something," Ilse said.

"I'm kind of busy with the local constabulary at the minute. Did you know that they carry *big* guns?"

"Stop fooling around, Jake," Anja said curtly. "Deal with it and get out of there before we lose the target and I fire your ass."

"Yes, ma'am."

Hawk looked at the policemen again as he put the Mercedes into reverse. Then after a brief wave, he floored the gas pedal and the vehicle shot backwards on the edge of control. After he'd gone twenty meters, Hawk spun the wheel and hit the brakes, allowing the front of the Mercedes to come around. Then he selected first gear and punched the gas once more.

The Brit felt the power flow through the vehicle and was pressed into the seat as the tires bit the pavement and propelled the Mercedes forward at an alarming rate.

Behind him the police officers opened fire and he heard the bullets punch into the vehicle's thin skin. Hawk climbed through the gears at a quick rate until the Mercedes was once again sitting on seventy. "I'm back mobile again, people. Point me in the right direction and turn me loose."

"Turn left and go straight until I tell you to stop," Ilse said.

"Roger that."

"You know, Jake, all this could have been avoided if you'd made the right choice at the restaurant," Anja said.

"Not my fault, ma'am," Hawk pointed out as he made the turn before bringing the Mercedes back up to speed. "I was just unlucky."

"You made a scene while you were on a mission."

"No, that was the other person who thought they recognized me from a time in North Africa."

"They did recognize you."

"Couldn't be helped."

"Could have if you had called her," Ilse pointed out.

Hawk changed a gear. "In my defense I was on a mission then."

"And used her in more than one way by the sound of it."

"Hang on a moment, are we trying to catch this tosser or conduct a character assassination?" Hawk protested.

"The second is good," Anja said. "Sounds well deserved to me."

"I agree," said Ilse.

"Shit."

Behind him, Hawk noticed the flashing lights. "I've still got a tail, by the way."

"I can see that," Ilse replied. "You've also got another coming in from the north and one more from the west."

"Did you say the north?"

"I did."

"But I'm going—"

"Yes, you are."

"Oh, bollocks."

Then he saw it. The lights, strobing off the buildings lining the street. He slowed, waiting to see what would happen. Hawk watched as it flew past him without stopping. He breathed a sigh of relief and then started to speed up again.

"Jake?"

It was Karl.

"What is it?"

"I'm intercepting a lot of chatter—"

"Yes, it will be the police," Hawk said, cutting him off.

"No, not police."

"Then who?"

"Jake, we've got vehicles coming in from the east. Not friendly."

It took a moment to digest Ilse's words but by the time he had, three vehicles had emerged from a side street he was passing and turned to follow. Two SUVs and a Humvee. "I've got them. Just get me closer to the target— Oh shit."

"Say again, Jake."

The night was suddenly lit by tracer rounds as the minigun on the Humvee opened fire. Hawk swerved left and then right as he tried to avoid the deadly fusillade. All around him the asphalt street seemed to lift in large chunks. He swung on the wheel again, coming back the other way.

"Jake, what's happening?" Ilse asked.

"I think our friend just called in the fucking cavalry."

———

OVERHEAD, in an armed Boeing MH-6M Little Bird helicopter, the pilot and his passenger watched the new developments unfold on the street below. Ilya Noskov, former Russian Spetsnaz colonel, said into his headset mic, "Viktor was right."

The tracers firing from the minigun looked like lances being thrown at the swerving vehicle.

Since Viktor Medvedev had lost his second in charge, and his best team, he had been quick to replace them with the former colonel and his hand-picked men. Medvedev was the man responsible for Anja losing half of her field team and setting off a bomb in Berlin, the result of which cost Anja her job with the intelligence service, furnishing her with nothing but acrimony towards the man.

The Mercedes was now weaving all over the street trying to avoid the incoming salvo of rounds. Noskov could see those slugs impacting from the bird's eye view he had, but none hit the speeding vehicle. Then he noticed the police cars closing in from behind them.

"Unit One, you have police behind you. Get rid of them."

The minigunner ceased firing ahead, spun around and began firing again behind them. Almost immediately the lead police vehicle exploded in a hurtling ball of flame, incinerating those within. The next one in line weaved desperately as it tried to avoid a collision with the wreck. In doing so he exposed himself to the fury of the incoming rounds from the six-barreled rotary machine gun.

The vehicle seemed to be torn apart. Holes opened in it like a giant block of Swiss cheese and all four tires blew out in quick succession. The windows went and the police officers inside were obliterated.

That left the last one which had wisely stopped its pursuit.

Noskov gave a satisfied grunt. "Now stop the damned car. Kill the one they call Hawk. A reward of fifty thousand Euros will go to the ones who do it." Then to the pilot, "Take us down."

CHAPTER TWO

Antwerp, Belgium

"OH, GOD NO," Ilse gasped as she saw the vehicles destroyed by the new arrivals. "Who are these people? Karl, find out what the hell is going on."

"On it already."

Anja's stare was transfixed on the screen. "Get emergency personnel dispatched immediately. Let the Belgian authorities know what's happening and that we have an ongoing operation in progress."

"Is that wise, ma'am?" Ilse asked.

"It is what it is. We'll deal with the fallout later. And get me Mister Harvey."

As she stared at the screen, she could see that the Mercedes was fast approaching a tight turn. She heard Ilse say. "Jake, right turn ahead. It'll put you back on track."

"Roger that." His voice was stiff.

Anja watched as Hawk made the turn. Behind him the armed vehicles were keeping pace. Ilse said, "All right, Jake, your target is five hundred meters ahead of you. You're back in the game."

And he was, right up until the first explosion from a

Hydra 70 rocket rocked the speeding Mercedes to its treads.

The orange fireball rose skyward in the darkness after its impact with the street. Ilse stared wide-eyed at the screen. "What was that?"

Karl answered her question. "That was a rocket. I've got a helicopter in the air. Looks like an MH-6."

Anja's head spun as she glared at her man. "How did that get past us?"

"We were expecting a police helicopter. That's what I thought it was."

"Damn it. Jake, can you hear me, over?"

"Yeah, I got you, boss. That one rattled a bit."

"Abort. I say again, abort. It's getting way out of hand."

"Roger that. Continuing mission."

Son of a bitch! "Jake, this is not the time—"

Then the next rocket hit, and things went pear-shaped.

———

HAWK FELT the explosion first then the mirror filled with the orange flame. Then came the thrust of concussive force followed by the rear end lifting. For a moment he felt a sense of weightlessness and then the Mercedes flipped forward and started skidding on its roof. Something which was all too familiar for the Talon field agent.

Hawk folded his arms across his chest and felt the airbag deploy. Sparks trailed behind the doomed vehicle until it slid to a stop.

For a moment, Hawk hung there in stunned silence, amazed that he was fine. The problem was, if he stayed where he was, he wouldn't be for very long.

"Jake?"

It was Ilse.

"Jake, talk to me. If you're still alive you need to get out of there now."

"I'm still in one piece, lass." He freed himself from the seatbelt. "Only just."

Crawling out through the window, he looked at the rear of the destroyed Mercedes. The pursuers were almost on top of him. He grabbed his SIG Sauer P226 from his waistband and started sprinting away from the wreck, keeping it between himself and the attackers.

"Jake, there's an alley about thirty meters ahead on your right. It's your best cover."

"Roger that."

Behind him he heard the vehicles stop and then loud voices. He glanced back and saw numerous armed men gathered around the Mercedes. A shout came, and then gunfire. Bullets whipped around Hawk as he ran. "Shit, not going to make it."

He darted to his right, straight towards a terraced café. It had a large window at its front with old-style writing marked across it. Hawk raised his SIG and fired three times. The window shattered and glass fell like confetti at a wedding. The Brit held his breath and leaped through the opening he'd made in the shopfront.

Having safely traversed it, he leaped over the counter and crouched down. The inside was dimly lit from the streetlamps out front. Hawk controlled his breathing so he could hear what was happening outside. At first it was the drumming beat of footsteps drawing near, then the voices.

"He went in here."

"Jake, whatever you're up to in there, you'd better have a good plan," Ilse said in his ear. "These people aren't going to muck around. X-ray closing your location."

Good girl. Hawk sucked in a breath and rose from behind the counter. He picked out his target and blew off two rounds, center mass. Found another target and did the same. Two down, shitloads more to go.

He pushed his luck and tried for a third, getting off another round before the pursuers opened fire forcing him to drop behind the counter again.

"Alpha Two, confirm two X-rays down, over?" Hawk's voice was clear and precise as he slipped into his Special Forces training.

"Confirm—"

An uptick in incoming fire shattered the store around him, causing him to miss the reply. "Say again, Alpha Two."

"Affirmative on the X-rays."

Bullets smacked into the wall above and behind him. Hawk glanced to his left and the end of the counter. On top of the polished countertop a jar full of round candy exploded and they rained down around the former SAS man who casually picked a piece up and put it in his mouth.

"Alpha Two, I need a way out of here."

"Jake, there looks to be a staircase to your left. It'll take you to the second floor and from there to the rooftop."

"And after I get up there?"

"Can't be any worse than where you are."

"Roger that."

Gathering himself, Hawk fired four more shots from the SIG and ran, head down, ass up. Bullets tracked him as he went. His gun arm rose as he ran, and he shot blindly out the opening. In front of himself, Hawk saw the turn into the alcove where the stairs started their climb.

He took them two at a time. Made the first turn where they doubled back, then continued to the landing. Hawk paused for a moment and looked down. He could hear the clamor of feet as the shooters continued the chase. The first one came into view, just a darkened shadow in the dim light.

Hawk blasted off four more shots, keeping a mental tally in his head. The lead shooter cried out and fell back into those following him. As the rest tried to free themselves from the tangle, the former SAS man climbed higher until he broke out onto the rooftop.

Even though it was dark, he could see that the only way was to his left where the terraced shops joined together with a flat, path-like strip across their rooftops lit by moonlight.

Hawk started running, leaping onto the pathway and across to the next tiled roof. Behind him the shouts sounded again, and it suddenly dawned on him that he was running a straight line.

"Oh, fuck!"

Without any hesitation he jumped from the rooftop path onto the tiles of the sloping roof. Immediately the tiles shifted under his feet and before he knew it, he was sliding down the slant towards the hard street below.

He tried to stop his descent by planting his feet firmly on the surface of the tiles but only succeeding in dislodging them. Before him, Hawk saw the gaping chasm open ready to swallow him whole like some hungry beast. Then he reached the tipping point and his feet passed over the precipice and beyond.

With one last act of desperation, he grasped at a television satellite dish fixed to the edge of the building. His left hand and finger locked around the metal pipe it was fixed to and he closed his eyes.

———

"WHERE DID HE GO?" Anja asked, staring at the screen, not trying to hide her look of concern.

"I'm not sure," Ilse replied sharing her commander's worry.

"Can we get another angle on that shot?"

"I'll try," Karl said.

"The shooters are on the rooftops closing in on the

area where Jake last was," Ilse said, her calm voice returning. "Bravo One, can you read me, over?"

"Read you loud and clear, Alpha Two." His voice sounded strained.

"Good to hear your voice, Jake. Where are you?"

"Oh, I'm just hanging around."

———

TO HIS SURPRISE the dish held and now he was suspended around fifteen meters above the street below. His left shoulder hurt but it could have been worse; he should be laying on the pavement below with several busted somethings.

"Not a good time to be hanging around, Bravo One. Suggest you keep moving, possibly n—"

The transmission was interrupted by the arrival of the Little Bird helicopter overhead. Hawk looked up and sighed. "You have to be fucking having a laugh. Shit a frigging brick."

From his precarious position, the former SAS man could see the shadow from the passenger side of the cockpit lean out. Then came the muzzle flashes followed by the cracks of bullets all around. Still with the SIG in his right hand, Hawk aimed at the MH-6 and fired back. "There, how's that, you fucking cock?"

He saw the helicopter flare and the pilot backed off instinctively.

"Jake, what's going on?" Anja asked.

"Some knob thinks he's frigging Rambo and is trying to shoot me from a helicopter. Remember how not long back I fell off a building?"

"Yes."

"Well, here goes nothing," Hawk said and let go—

—falling all of two meters onto a balcony with a small outdoor table and chairs on it.

Hawk crashed through the table, shattering its wood into kindling. He rolled over, groaned, and came to his feet. He could still hear the helicopter overhead and he knew that the shooters wouldn't be far away. The longer his plight progressed, the more it felt like some first-person shooter game where everything gets thrown at you towards the end. Except the worst possible outcome for him was death; there was no going back and starting again to achieve some feat.

The former SAS operative came to his feet. He staggered to the rail and looked down. Maybe—more gunfire.

"Bollocks," he growled and threw himself over the rail.

For once, he landed right. Feet first, knees together, roll. Hurt like a bitch but he was still good. He looked to his left and ran along the street, using the shadows for cover. He ducked into a doorway and pressed his back hard against the door. He waited for a moment as the helicopter above circled then moved away before he came out and kept going. "Alpha Two, copy?"

"Copy, Bravo One. We've lost you on our screen."

"I'm moving east along some street. I can see an alley up further on the right, I'll try to make it. Wait one."

Glancing left and right to make sure it was all clear, Hawk ran across the street and into the shadows on the other side. He then made for the alley which was thirty meters further on.

Once inside the mouth, Hawk paused. "Alpha One, I have a theory."

"Please enlighten us, Bravo One."

"I'm thinking that these people don't belong to Erkens. He doesn't have enough backing for something like this."

"Yes, agreed."

"Which leaves just one man, possibly two."

"I'm listening," Anja replied.

"Well, it could be Hakim Anwar."

"Yes, but he wouldn't know we were coming after him."

"Or it could be our old friend Medvedev."

Anja considered the theory for a moment before saying, "Get me a prisoner."

"I'll do what I can, boss, but I'm a little outnumbered and outgunned."

"Field interrogation," Anja shot back at him.

"If you say so."

"Do it."

Setting his jaw firm, Hawk slipped back further into the darkened alley, and waited.

———

THEY TOOK THEIR TIME, but eventually they made it to his alley. Searching every nook and cranny along the way. In the distance the sound of sirens was getting closer. He heard voices before two men appeared in the alley mouth. They hesitated before walking in. Hawk heard one of them mention something about money. Some kind of reward.

Hawk crouched behind a large trash bin on rollers. He'd shifted it out to make room enough for him to fit and as the two shooters approached, he slipped in behind it.

A cursory glance was all the pair gave the back side of the trash bin as they walked past. Just pure laziness on their part. But that was fine by Hawk. Coming out behind them he crept up close like a cat stalking prey. Hawk brought the butt of the handgun down violently on the back of one shooter's head, sending him collapsing with a grunt mid stride. His friend gave out a strangled squawk of alarm as he turned to see what had happened. The Brit hit him in the jaw. A solid blow, enough to put him down, but not sufficient to knock him out cold.

Hawk knelt beside the fallen shooter and pressed the

barrel of his gun into his forehead. "You hear me, twat features?"

The man moaned.

"I'll take that as yes. Listen up. Who the fuck are you working for?"

No answer.

Hawk clipped him with the gun. "Come on, mate, speak up. I'm fucking deaf from all that shooting you pricks were doing at me."

"Fuck you," he groaned, his voice heavily accented.

Russian. "You working for Medvedev? Is that it?"

"Suck your cock," the man ground out.

Hawk grinned bitterly. "That's suck my cock." Then he pressed the muzzle of the SIG hard against the killer's right thigh and pulled the trigger.

The gun kicked in his hand as the round punched through flesh and bone. The shot was muffled but the howl escaping the man's lips was anything but. Hawk rapidly clamped a hand over the noisome orifice and hissed, "Shut up! Shut the fuck up! Now tell me who you work for."

The man writhed in pain and managed to get out, "Ilya Noskov."

"Who does he work for?"

"I—I don't know."

Hawk shot him again. Muffled screams tried to burst past Hawk's hand, but he squeezed harder. He leaned in close and said, "Speak, or I'll fucking shoot you again."

"Medusa."

The former SAS man nodded and shot him in the head before getting quickly to his feet and hurrying deeper into the ally. "Alpha One, copy?"

"Copy, Bravo One."

"Did you get that?"

"Yes," came the grim reply.

"I'm done here. I'll see you when I get back."

"See you then."

——————

ANJA TURNED TO FACE KARL. She took her headset off and said, "Find Erkens. We still have a mission to finish."

"Yes, boss."

Turning, she looked across to see Ilse staring at her. "What is it?"

"Are we going to talk about what just happened?"

"What do you mean? What just happened?"

"The fact that Jake just tortured a man in the field to get answers from him."

Anja shook her head. "That's not considered torture, Ilse. It was aggressive questioning."

"I thought we were better than that," Ilse replied.

"Maybe once upon a time we were. But that was a different life. Before Medvedev killed our friends. This isn't going to be a job for the faint of heart. Not if we want to see it all the way through. Lives depend on the answers we get. If you can't deal with that then I won't hold it against you if you want to depart the team. But you need to think about it and make a decision quickly. If we are to replace you, we need to start looking now."

Ilse stared at her and said, "I'll do that."

"Good. Now, get Jake back here for some rest before he goes back out. Meanwhile, I've got some people with ruffled feathers to smooth over."

It was another hour before Hawk returned to their base of operations. "Where are we at?" he asked Anja when he saw her.

She was talking to Grizz Harvey, the big, broad-chested, six-foot-five former special operator with the bushy black beard and shaved head. He took one look at

23

Hawk and winced. Then he said, "I hear you've been wrecking vehicles and jumping off buildings again."

"Oh, I think you left out getting shot at by helicopters."

"Man, you attract trouble like flies to horse shit."

"Like your beard, huh?"

"Something like that. Good to see you're all right, brother."

"How are you feeling, Jake?" Anja asked.

"I'll live. What I'd like to know is how Medusa knew we'd be going after Erkens." He looked towards Karl. "Can you find out all you can about Ilya Noskov?"

"Working on it as we speak."

"Good man."

Hawk walked over to where Karl was seated and looked over his shoulder as he worked. Anja called over to him, "I still need to talk to you, Jake."

"I won't be too hard to locate," he called back in his best John Wayne drawl.

———

12 Hours Later

Anja waited patiently for the screen to come on and the video feed to come through. When it eventually did, she was staring at a ragged-looking Leonid Federov. Upon seeing her his eyes seemed to brighten. "Well, if it isn't my favorite German, Anja Meyer. How are you?"

"Skip the pleasantries, Leonid. I'm only after information. That's all you are here for."

He gave her a fake smile. "I always aim to please."

"Where might Dedrick Erkens go to hide?"

"Hmm, I'm not sure. Why would you ask me that—unless you missed him the first time?"

"Just tell me, Leonid."

"Oh, you did miss him." He chuckled.

"Enough of the theatrics, Leonid, or I'll have your minders take all of your privileges away."

His stare hardened as he scoffed, "What privileges?"

"You're alive, let's start with that one."

Leonid sighed. "You're no fun."

"I'm not here for fun, remember?"

"Oh, very well. Where did you lose him?"

"Antwerp."

"He will go to Luxembourg."

"Are you sure?"

"Yes, he has a place there that he visits. He thinks no one knows about it, but Viktor knows everything."

"Then that's where we'll go."

"Be careful. He has men everywhere."

"So does Viktor. It seems he's already replaced you."

"Really? With who?"

"Ilya Noskov."

Federov nodded. "I'm impressed. Noskov is a good soldier."

"Where in Luxembourg?" Anja asked.

"There is an estate on the outskirts. He will go there."

"Give everything you know to your minders. They will send it to me."

"What do I get in return?" Federov asked.

"You get to live."

CHAPTER THREE

Luxembourg, 24 Hours Later, Interpol Safehouse

"HOW MANY ROOMS IN THAT THING?" Hawk asked as he stared at the screen.

Beside him, Harvey said, "Too many to clear them all."

Hawk nodded. "We need to pinpoint him somehow."

The picture kept changing. Erkens was indeed there but so was at least a dozen-man security team. All armed to the teeth. "He's got some well-armed friends," Hawk pointed out.

The pictures kept changing.

"Stop!" Karl snapped.

"You see a dirty picture, Karl?" Hawk asked.

"Very funny," Karl shot back at him. "What do you see?"

"A picture of a woman in a maid's uniform," Hawk replied.

"Someone's been playing kinky dress ups," Harvey said.

"Grow up, you two," Ilse reprimanded them. "What you see there is intel on legs. If anyone can pinpoint

Erkens in the mansion, it's her. Karl, find out who she is and where she lives."

"Yes, ma'am."

Karl went off to do his work and left the other three where they were. Ilse stared at them both, a stern expression on her face. "When will you two learn?"

Hawk gave her an innocent look. "What?"

"It's all him," Harvey said, indicating Hawk with his thumb.

"Just take it easy on him. He's a good officer."

Hawk nodded. "All right, I'll start tomorrow."

"What's wrong with today?"

"Someone might have changed some of the keys around on his computer."

Harvey's face went red as he tried not to burst out laughing. Ilse leapt to her feet. "Damn it, Jake, you're a bloody child."

She stormed off looking for Karl. Harvey finally couldn't hold it in anymore and let the laughter out. "You're a mad bastard, Jake."

"Not as mad as what she is."

"Going to be a big job getting the target out of there," Harvey said to Hawk as he stared at the screen.

"Yeah, I might need someone to watch my back."

"You asking?"

"Yeah, I think I am. Just you. We don't want too many blundering around in there. If the balloon goes up too early, we'll lose him again. I don't think the boss will like that."

"I'm game," Harvey said.

Hawk picked up a picture from the coffee table. "It looks like they have security cameras on the walls. If we can get in here and avoid the guards, we should be good. We might need to take out the guard at the pool."

Harvey nodded but the look on his face told Hawk he was still concerned about something.

27

"What is it?" Hawk asked.

"Those two guards on the rooftop of the mansion. We may have to neutralize both threats."

"All right so we'll take Nemo. He can deal with them."

"Sounds good to me."

Suddenly Karl appeared and Hawk could see that he wasn't happy. The former SAS man came to his feet just as Karl threw a looping right which crashed against Hawk's jaw. The Brit went down onto his buttocks. He looked up at Karl who stood over him. The former German intelligence officer glared at him. "You had that coming, *schweinhund*."

Hawk dabbed at the corner of his mouth with the back of his hand. He gave a nod and said, "You know what, Karl, you're right. I had that coming."

The Brit reached out with his right hand for Karl to take and help him up. The German hesitated then took it, hauling Hawk up off his ass.

"I'm sorry, Karl, it won't happen again. Are we good?"

Karl nodded hesitantly but said, "Yes."

Watching Karl walk away until he disappeared, Hawk turned to Harvey and said, "That felt like he hit me with a fucking hammer."

"Looked that way."

"At least now we know," Hawk told him.

"Know what?"

"That he can take care of himself."

Harvey shook his head. "You're a fucking idiot."

Hawk grinned and then winced. "Yeah, but I'm a smart idiot."

"Fuck off."

———

HAWK WATCHED as the perimeter guard jerked and dropped into an untidy heap on the damp grass he'd been walking. "X-ray down."

"Roger that," Hawk whispered in acknowledgement of Nemo's voice in his ear. "We're moving."

The intel from the maid had come through that Erkens spent most of his time in a library on the second floor.

After crossing the high stone wall to break through the perimeter, Hawk and Harvey had crouched in the shadows of the bushes while Nemo Kent took out the first of the roving guards with a single shot.

Keeping to the shadows the pair advanced to a point where they halted and waited for the next guard to approach.

He made slow progress, almost disinterested in the task at hand. It was something which cost him his life as he reached where Hawk was hiding in the shadows. With his combat knife in his right hand, the Brit imitated a silent wraith rising from the depths of Hell. The razor-edged blade slid easily across the guard's throat just after the operator's left hand clamped the mouth to prevent the escape of any cries.

Hawk cast him aside and let him fall to the ground. Then he brought his MP5SD back up to his shoulder and began stepping across the open ground. He made it halfway before floodlights lit up the yard and an alarm started wailing.

"Fuck it," Hawk growled "That's torn it."

"What the hell did you do?" Harvey asked almost casually.

"Frigging motion sensors. Didn't consider that, did we."

He was suddenly aware of a shooter appearing to his left. The MP5 came around and spat twice. The guard threw up his arms and fell back.

"Moving," Hawk snapped. "Nemo, the bastards on the roof."

"On it, Birdman."

The Brit glanced at Harvey. "Birdman?"

"Don't like it?"

"Not a fan," Hawk replied as he pushed forward towards the pool area.

"Two X-rays down up top," Nemo reported over their comms.

"Pool guy," Harvey shot back at him.

"Down."

"Grizz, go right," Hawk said. "Hook around the side in case our rabbit tries to run."

"On my way," Harvey said.

"Talk to me, Bravo One," Ilse said over the comms.

"Bravo Two set off a motion sensor, Alpha Two," Hawk said as he hurried up some sandstone stairs that topped out on the paved pool area. He grinned. He could imagine the big American shaking his head. "Do we have any movement out the front?"

"Negative at the moment."

"Copy."

Hawk crossed the pool area, walking past the fallen guard whose blood had formed a large red halo around his head. The Brit stopped at the French doors momentarily. "Bravo One is breaching."

"Roger, Bravo One."

Stepping back, Hawk lifted his foot to slam his boot onto the wood just below the lock when the glass in front of him exploded outward, shattered by bullets. He cried out in pain and fell backward, landing heavily onto the pavers.

AS INDICATED BY HAWK, Grizz Harvey circled to the right running into another perimeter guard along the way. Firing while on the move Grizz dropped the guard on a patch of grass that had likely been crossed countless times already that night by the security team. As he stepped over him, he put a bullet into the man's head.

When Harvey approached the corner of the building, a vehicle was slowing to a halt on the turnaround.

The interior light came on as the driver's door opened and an armed man climbed out. He began walking past the hood towards the steps leading up to the house. The suppressed Bren2 in Harvey's hands rattled, and the man dropped on the spot.

As Harvey passed the downed man, he put one more into the chest. Then he climbed the stairs and stopped at the front door.

Suddenly his comms lit up. "Jake's down! Jake's down at the rear of the building."

"Shit," Harvey muttered to himself. "Nemo, can you get a line on the front?"

"Affirmative, Grizz."

"If we have any squirters, take them down."

"Copy. Where are you going?"

"Inside."

Harvey kicked the door hard, sending it crashing back against the wall on its hinges. Not waiting for the rebound he stepped around the moving door, sweeping back and forth with his weapon, making sure that the entrance was clear.

On the stairs a shooter suddenly appeared, and he switched up his eye and dropped him with two well placed shots before the guard could open fire. The big man started walking through the house, continuing a sweeping motion as he went, then spoke into his radio, "Hawk, you got me, buddy?"

Nothing but static came back to him, so he tried again. "Jake, you there, over?"

"Fuck." The voice was etched with pain.

"Talk to me, buddy."

Another shooter appeared ahead of Harvey in the hallway. The weapon in his hand spat twice more, and the man jerked violently before falling to the floor with a clatter of gun on tile. Stepping over the body, he walked through a doorway leading into the kitchen. "Jake, where are you?"

"The landing out near the pool. I think it's off the living room."

Giving the kitchen one last cursory look, Harvey about faced, then walked back out into the hallway. Halfway along it, he turned right into a branch which he hoped would take him in the right direction.

With his Bren still up at his shoulder, the hallway opened out into a large living area. He caught movement to his right, brought the weapon around, and fired a short burst. Another shooter went down.

Harvey glanced around the room and saw the shattered French doors. And then he saw the lump lying just outside on the hard surface, rolling around as though he'd been kicked in the balls.

The big man stepped outside and knelt beside Hawk. "You OK, Jake?"

"Fucking bollocks," he groaned. "Took a couple of rounds to the chest plate, but I guess I'll be OK."

Harvey helped him to his feet and said, "You know how we didn't want to sweep this house?

"Don't bloody remind me," Hawk growled.

"The HVT is in there somewhere."

"Roger that."

Hurrying back inside the house, the pair was met by a chaotic fusillade of gunfire. They took cover before Hawk brought the shooter down with a well-aimed burst.

"We need to get upstairs," Hawk grated as a wave of pain swept through his chest.

Moving back towards the front of the house and the open stairwell there, they hit the stairs and surged upward.

A shooter appeared at the top on the landing and Harvey rapidly put him down. Continuing to the top, they stepped over the body and moved quickly into the hallway sweeping as they went. "The room at the end," Hawk said.

A door burst open to Hawk's right and a figure slammed into him, pinning his weapon between them as they struggled. The assailant punched Hawk in the face, drawing blood and dislodging the NVGs. The pair grappled with each other until the former SAS man reached for his sidearm. Hawk drove it into the man's ribs and fired twice. The man howled in pain and fell away.

As soon as he hit the floor, Hawk shot him again. "Asshole."

Meanwhile at the end of the hallway, Harvey had breached the room and gunfire could be heard. Hawk hurried to enter and found Harvey down on one knee, a gunman standing over him.

Upon seeing the threat, Hawk fired, and the gunman fell beside the stricken Talon operator. Glancing to his right he saw the HVT. "Don't you fucking move."

"Who are you?"

Hawk ignored him and went to his fallen comrade. "You should have waited, buddy."

"Yeah, I know," Harvey grunted. "I fucked up."

"Alpha One, I need EMS now. We have a Bravo element down." Hawk looked at the wound.

"Say your last, Bravo One."

"Grizz is down. He's Cat Two at this time but it could go Cat One if he keeps bleeding like this. Break. Nemo, get your ass in here."

"On my way, Bravo One."

"Bravo One, Alpha One, EMS are on their way."

"Roger that."

He looked down at Harvey who was growing pale. "Hang in there, buddy, help is on the way."

The big man chuckled. "You know, it doesn't matter how many times I get shot, it still frigging hurts."

"Isn't that the truth?"

CHAPTER FOUR

Luxembourg, Interpol Safehouse

"I'VE STOOD Mister Harvey's team down," Anja told Hawk as she entered the room where Ilse was checking him over. "MacBride still isn't one-hundred percent and now we have their commander down."

"MacBride is fine. He was out in the field—"

"And he shouldn't have been," Anja snapped. "Neither should you have. We all needed down time but here we are, hard at it again. Harvey's team works as a well-oiled machine when they're all fit. Right now, their commander will be in the hospital for at least a week."

"That bad?"

"No, it could have been worse."

Hawk stared at Anja and waited for her to continue. When she didn't, he asked, "Are we going to talk to the prisoner?"

She nodded. "Yes shortly."

"What are we waiting for then?"

"A visitor."

Hawk was about to ask her who when the visitor appeared. Former General Mary Thurston entered the room with purposeful strides. "Hello, Anja, Mister Hawk, how are we?"

"We are very well, thank you, ma'am," Anja said with a glare at Hawk before he could speak. "Did you have a good flight?"

It had been Mary Thurston who was responsible for putting the team together. When Hank Jones requested that she put a team together to fight Medusa and their trafficking ring, she went to work and found people fit for the job, with a little help from a couple of her own team. What she ended up with was a bunch of misfits nobody wanted. But they were damned good at what they did.

"How is our friend Mister Harvey this morning?" Thurston asked.

"The doctor has him laid up for at least a week," Anja replied.

The former general, gave Hawk a once over. "And you, Mister Hawk, how are you doing?"

"I'm just fine, General."

"Does someone want to fill me in on what happened last evening?" Thurston asked.

Hawk said, "It went like every mission that doesn't survive first contact, ma'am."

"Really? How about you tell me?"

Hawk sighed. "We inserted under the cover of darkness. We had an overwatch in position. We took out a couple of the guards and then somewhere along the way the bastards had a motion sensor installed. Things went downhill after that. It was shoot and clear as we went."

"Keep going."

"Harvey and I split up. One went round the front, which was Harvey, and I went round the back. Just as I was about to enter, I got shot in the chest plate. Meanwhile, Harvey came in through the front door. Worked his way to the back where I was down. Once he had me on my feet, we moved upstairs along the hallway towards the room where the HVT was supposedly hiding. I got hit from a side door by an X-ray who just charged out and pinned me. Then—"

"Wait a moment," Thurston said. "Weren't you clearing rooms as you went?"

"No, ma'am, there wasn't time. Besides, there were too many of them."

"Tell me what happened next." The general's face was grim.

"I killed the X-ray and then followed Harvey in through the door at the end of the hallway where the HVT was."

"He didn't wait for you."

"No, ma'am, he didn't."

Thurston frowned. "Not a smart move."

Hawk nodded. "No, ma'am, but I would have done exactly the same thing in that situation."

"All right, what happened next?"

"When I entered the room, Grizz was already down. There was an X-ray standing over him about to shoot him. I shot the X-ray and then cleared the rest of the room, noticing the HVT was there in the corner. After the room was secure, I called in for a medevac and then saw to Grizz. And that's it."

"And what did you learn?"

It was Hawk's turn to frown. "Ma'am?"

"It's a simple enough question, Jake. What did you learn from the operation?"

Hawk said, "I'm not doing this, ma'am, you weren't there, you don't know. Unless you were on the operation, you can't judge what we did. And if you want to know, would I do it all over again the exact same way? The answer is yes."

"Fair enough, Jake. That will be all."

Hawk left the room, leaving Thurston alone with Anja and Ilse. "I'm getting a lot of government noise from this latest operation. I'm not going to judge how you've conducted it, but a little more under the radar would be nice."

"I agree," said Anja. "However, Medvedev is a very capable foe."

Thurston walked across the room and stared out a window. "Tell me why you were after Erkens."

Ilse said, "We believe he has information into a terrorist camp in the Nubian Desert. That information being the precise position of it."

"In that camp," said Anja, "there are some girls who were shipped to them by Medusa. We're trying to get them out before they disappear forever. And to get that location, we have to get Erkens to cooperate."

"And has he yet?"

"We were just about to question him when you arrived."

Thurston nodded. "Let's get started then, shall we?"

"If it's all the same with you, Mary, I'd like Jake to do the interrogation. We can observe. We'll have a camera and a microphone set up in the room."

"It's fine by me."

"Good. Let's get started. Ilse, get Jake. Tell him I need him to get his nasty side on."

"I'm sure that will not be a problem."

———

"CAN I WATERBOARD HIM?" asked Hawk.

"No."

"Can I shoot him in the leg?"

"Jake, be serious," Anja said.

"I was being serious," he shot back at her, wondering why she thought he was kidding.

"Just get the answers we need. That's all you have to do."

"I'd still like to shoot him."

"Jake!"

"Fine."

Hawk turned away and walked to the door that led into the interrogation room. Pulling it closed it behind him as he stepped through, he stopped and stared at the man sitting handcuffed behind the table. He stood holding the pose like a statue for what seemed like an age before crossing the room and taking a chair that was opposite Erkens.

After he'd sat down, Jake took out his SIG P226 and set it on the table. "She told me I couldn't waterboard you or shoot you in the leg. She didn't say nothing about your bollocks and by Christ, boy, I will shoot you in the fucking things if you don't answer my questions."

In the other room, Anja looked at Mary Thurston. She said, "He's right. I didn't say he couldn't shoot him in his balls."

"Who are you?" Erkens asked.

"It don't matter who I am. But we know who you are. And who you work for?"

"I work for nobody. I work for myself. I am a shipping contractor."

"And if I was an innocent teenager who wasn't wise to the ways of the world, Dedrick, I might well believe you. But I'm not and I don't. So, let's start again. Tell me about Hakim Anwar."

"Don't know him."

Hawk smiled. Not a warm pleasant smile, a cold, humorless one. "See, this is how interrogation works. At first, I ask you questions that I know the answer to so I can tell when you're lying. Then I ask others, throwing the occasional one in that I know. And right at this point I know that you are *fucking lying!*"

Erkens flinched as Hawk's voice went up. Then he said, "I don't—"

Hawk's hand lashed out, slapping him across the face. "I don't have time for this, right. Answer the questions or I am going to shoot you."

The shock of the blow started to wear off and Erkens finally realized the predicament he was in. He nodded and said, "Ask your questions."

A few moments later, the door opened and Ilse entered. She sat beside Hawk in the second chair on that side. "Shall we start?"

Hawk nodded. "Tell me about Hakim Anwar."

"What do you want to know?"

"What do you do for him?"

"I move things for him."

"Can you be more specific?" Ilse asked.

"Products, items. Things like that."

"What about girls?" Hawk asked.

Erkens nodded. "Sometimes."

"He buys them, and you ship them? Is that what you do?"

"Sometimes."

Ilse asked, "Is that a yes, or no? I'm thinking it's a yes."

"If you know the answer, why ask the question?" Erkens asked.

"Because it's all about what answers you're giving us," Hawk replied. "Because if you lie I'm going to smash you in the face."

"Where do you usually pick them up from?" Ilse asked.

"It depends on where he purchases them. I'm like a middleman. Once he buys the merchandise, he comes to me and then I find customers, unless they've already come to me. Then he will buy the product."

"But there's only one place he can buy the girls from, isn't there?" Hawk said.

Erkens nodded. "If you want to live, yes."

"And that's from Viktor Medvedev."

There was a frown that appeared on Erken's face. "From who?"

"Viktor Medvedev. Also known as the man in charge of Medusa."

"I don't know about that. The only one I ever saw from the other side was—what was his name? Leonid Fedorov."

"Medusa's front and center man. Like a PR agent," Hawk said.

"If that's how you want to put it."

"Who were the people in Antwerp? The ones in the helicopter and the others in the armed vehicles?" Hawk asked him.

"I don't know, they just appeared."

Hawk's eyes narrowed. "Are you sure about that?"

"Yes."

"Does the name Ilya Noskov ring a bell?" Ilse asked.

There was recognition in the man's eyes at the name. He knew he hadn't got away with trying to cover it up so he nodded and came clean. "Yes, he's former Russian special forces. Hires out to the highest bidder. I heard Medusa was chasing him after their last team was taken out."

"So they just go out and hire whoever they want. Is that it?"

"That's not how it is. Well, it is in a way, but once you're in, there is no out unless you're dead."

Hawk leaned closer and gave the man a hard stare, as though daring him not to tell the truth. "How is it that you know so much but you can't tell me who the leader of Medusa is? You lying to me, Dedrick?"

"No. I'm actually surprised that you know who it is. Medusa revels in the world of secrecy. It lives on the dark side. If anyone ever knew, they would just kill them."

Ilse said. "Let's get back to you, shall we? Not so long ago you shipped some girls for Anwar to a terrorist

41

camp in the Nubian Desert. We want to know where that is."

Dedrick's face was full of fear. "I can't tell you that, they will kill me."

"I'll fucking kill you if you don't tell us," Hawk snarled viciously.

"You don't understand that they can get to me anywhere."

"I understand, alright. But if you don't tell us, I'll see you put in a prison in general population where anybody can get at you."

"Who are the terrorists?" Ilse asked.

"They call themselves the North African Freedom Fighters. They are responsible for bombings in Cairo, Benghazi, Yemen., Jordan, and a couple of ones in Europe, mainly one in Austria and another in Greece."

"I think I've heard of them," Hawk said.

"Every time they do something, more people flock to their banner. Soon they will become what ISIS was to Syria and Iraq. There is a village where the training camp is based. They killed all the villagers there and moved in. It has the only well for hundreds of miles. That is how they can stay there."

"Can you show me on a map?" Hawk asked.

"Yes."

Hawk grabbed his handgun and left the room to find what he needed. Meanwhile, Ilse asked more questions. "What will they do with the girls?"

He stared at her, not answering.

Ilse tried again. "What will they do with the girls?"

Again he said nothing.

She knew what he was up to. It was obvious that he was scared of Hawk, but because she was a woman...

With swift movements she drew her own weapon and used it to club him on the side of his head. "Listen, you piece of *scheisse*, just because you have no respect for women doesn't mean they will take your fucking crap."

Blood ran down the side of Erkens's head. Anger flared in his eyes as he snarled, "If I wasn't in these cuffs I would—"

She hit him in the mouth, making him slump back. Then she dug into her pocket for a key, before releasing the cuffs.

Inside the other room, Thurston lurched to her feet at the sight of it. "What the hell?"

Anja grabbed her arm. "Wait."

In the room, Erkens reared up and came around the table. "Stinking whore."

Ilse grinned wickedly. "If I was, asshole, I'd have all your money."

He swung a wild, uncoordinated blow which she avoided with ease. Then she stepped in close and hit him in the face. It rocked him where he stood but his adrenaline was flowing, and he stepped forward to continue his assault.

Another wild blow, easily avoided, countered by a straight right to the trafficker's throat. This one got his attention. Erkens stiffened and staggered back. However, Ilse wasn't finished with him. She twisted on the spot, bringing her right leg up, power driving through her hips. The boot she wore—heavy and hard—caught the trafficker on the side of the jaw. At the last moment she pulled it; after all, there was no use of a prisoner with a broken jaw.

Erkens still went down, blood flowing from his mouth. He lay there moaning with Ilse standing over him. "You were saying?"

The door opened and Hawk walked in with a map. He looked at Erkens and then at Ilse. "Did I miss something?"

"Get him up, Jake," Ilse said. "If I do it, I might actually break his jaw this time."

After Erkens was upright and seated once more, Hawk sat down and unfurled the map in front of them on the table. "Show me where it is."

———

"ALL THE GIRLS ARE THERE?" Hawk asked.

Erkens nodded. "At least four of them will be. Maybe five."

Ilse frowned. "What do you mean?"

"Medusa gave their leader, Mustafa Osman, a bonus."

"Stop talking in riddles. Tell me." Ilse was swiftly losing patience again.

"Polly White. Does the name mean anything to you?"

"I'm going to break his frigging neck, Jake," Ilse growled.

Hawk stared at him. "Stop frigging around, you twat. Or I'm going to rip your bollocks off and stuff them down your throat."

Erkens sighed, trying to make out that he had all the power. "Polly White is the daughter of British MP, George White."

Hawk stared at the camera.

On the outside, Anja turned to Thurston. "Why don't we know this?"

Thurston stood up. "I'll find out."

Ilse said, "You're telling us that a British MP's daughter is a prisoner with these terrorists?"

"If she is still alive," Erkens replied with a tone, but not brave enough to smirk.

"Why would Medusa do that?"

"A month ago, British SAS raided a camp in northern Sudan. Osman's wife was there. She was accidentally killed in the crossfire, so now he wants revenge."

"Was she directly targeted?" asked Hawk. "Polly White, I mean."

Erkens shrugged. "It seems too much of a coincidence for her not to have been."

Hawk looked at Ilse and indicated towards the door. They went outside and found Anja waiting for them. Ilse said, "If this happened a month ago, then our friend should know all about it."

Anja nodded. "That's just what I was thinking."

––––––––

FIVE MINUTES LATER, Anja was sitting in front of a laptop staring at the multi-colored face of Leonid Federov via Zoom. He smiled at her and said, "What do I owe the pleasure?" His voice nasally from the swelling of his broken nose from their last encounter.

"I assure you, Leonid, it is no pleasure looking at your face," Anja sneered.

"Such harsh words from a pretty lady."

"Tell me about Polly White, Leonid."

The man's face changed. "Oh, dear."

"Oh, dear is right. Now speak."

"Polly White was targeted specifically with Mustafa Osman in mind. He reached out through a mutual friend requesting that we find someone for him, who fit specific criteria. When the details came out that his wife had been killed by the British, the girl had to be British and must be important. Polly White just happened to be in the wrong place at the right time."

"Where was that?" Anja asked.

"In Brussels. We passed her on to Anwar because he already had a shipment going to Osman. It all fell into place perfectly."

Anja glared at him. "What do they plan to do with her?"

"I don't know. Ransom her, kill her, both. Maybe sell her to the highest bidder. She's quite pretty. She'd command a large price. Then she would just disappear into the darkness."

Unwilling to listen to more, Anja disconnected the call.

When she met back up with the others, Thurston had news. "Polly White was indeed taken from Brussels. Her kidnapping has been kept quiet."

"She was deliberately targeted in retaliation for the death of Mustafa Osman's wife," Anja supplied. "But why was it kept quiet?"

"Because they paid the ransom, but the deal was reneged on and they never got her back."

Ilse said, "So she still could be there, or she could be dead."

"Yes, on both counts."

Hawk said, "What's the plan?"

Anja stared at him. "Come up with one. Bring it to me and then we'll see. By the way, you'll be going in alone."

———

ILSE, Hawk, and Karl pored over the maps and intelligence for three hours while they cobbled together a plan they thought could work. Then they took it to Anja.

Hawk pointed at a spot on the map about 5 miles from the village. "I get dropped here with a dirt bike and then I ride it as close as I can before going in on foot. I'll wait until dark before taking a look around, see if I can find them. If I do, I plan on trying to bring them out, but I'm going to need exfil almost immediately."

Anja nodded. "We can get you a helicopter. That's not a problem. Have you thought about what you'll do if things go wrong?"

"That's all I have thought about," Hawk replied.

Thurston looked at Hawk. "I know your team is down. Do you need anyone? I might be able to detail Reaper."

Hawk shook his head. "I'll be fine. Probably better if I do it alone. As long as my exfil is close by, I can get them out."

"You're either crazy or you have a death wish," Thurston said.

"Didn't you know, all us Limeys are crazy?"

She nodded resignedly. "I work with one, remember?"

Hawk smiled. "Perhaps craziest one of the lot."

Thurston sighed. "Fine, I'll leave you to it. Let me know if you need anything."

"Yes, ma'am," Anja said.

Before she left, Thurston stared at Hawk. "One more thing. Try to stop stealing expensive cars. It costs money."

Hawk grinned. "What can I say? I have expensive taste."

After Thurston had left, Anja called them around once more. "We'll operate out of Djibouti. We'll be able to get a drone to help and fly air support. After Jake is inserted, the Chinook will stay on the ground unless there is a direct threat."

"Sounds good to me."

"Jake, if we have to abort under any circumstances, you get out. Understood?"

"Yes, boss."

"Even without the girls."

"There is one problem which I foresee," Karl said.

"What is that?" Anja asked, interested in gaining as much insight as possible.

"If the girls are being used as wives for the terrorists, then they're not all going to be located in the one spot."

"Why didn't you bring this up before?" Hawk growled.

"You never asked."

"Shit a bloody brick. Am I meant to think of everything?"

"What's the terrain like around the camp?" Anja inquired.

"There are a couple of low ridges and a formation of rocks to the north," replied Hawk.

"Then you lay up for at least twenty-four hours before you go in."

"You're forgetting about the helicopter."

"It can come off site and be put back into play when it's required," Anja said.

Hawk shook his head. "No good."

"Then what do you suggest?"

"I have no idea," he said with a shrug of his shoulders, rolling his head to both sides to stretch his neck.

"Fine, then we go with what I said."

"Yes, ma'am."

CHAPTER FIVE

Nubian Desert, Sudan

THE KAWASAKI 600 dirt bike handled well across the rough terrain and Hawk was more than pleased. His kit was attached to the back, with his Bren2 affixed to the handlebars at the front.

Dodging a formation of rust-colored rocks he rode around a couple of small knolls in front of him.

"You've got about a mile to go, Bravo One," Ilse said into his comms. "You might want to think about ditching the bike. You know how noise travels across the desert."

"Roger that."

Slowing the bike to a halt, he parked it before unloading his equipment. He looked at the bike. It seemed to be a waste to abandon the thing. He'd quite enjoyed riding it. Still, it wasn't his money.

Now he continued on foot. It was hot, almost suffocating, but his SAS training helped him cope. Twenty minutes later, he found his layup position and settled in for the long haul.

———

HAWK SCANNED the village with the binoculars from beneath the camo netting he had draped above him. As he commenced another sweep with them, he paused. "Alpha Two, can we get a look at the hut on the left side of the village? I've got an X-ray standing talking to a woman with a bowl of food."

"Copy, Bravo One. Give me a minute."

It was late in the afternoon and so far, Hawk had been able to locate ten women who, by all appearances, were foreign nationals. As he observed the pair, one of the men broke away and disappeared into the hut, reappearing several heartbeats later without the food.

"Bravo One, copy?"

"I'm here."

"ISR shows an unknown inside the hut. It could be that this is the package."

"Are you able to determine whether it is male or female, Alpha Two?"

"Negative at this time."

"Shit." Then he realized something. They had started referring to 'the package' over the past few transmissions. "Alpha Two, is there something I need to know?"

"Not that I'm aware of, Bravo."

"Put the boss on."

"I'm here, Jake," Anja replied.

"What's this package bullshit?" he asked, keeping his cool.

"The mission has been re-tasked, Bravo."

"The hell it has."

"I'm not going to argue with you, Jake. Polly White is the mission. Once you have her clear, a heavy SAS team will be inserted to rescue the others."

"I guess money and power speak louder than words," Hawk growled in a low voice. "When were you going to fucking tell me?"

"I don't like that tone, Jake. Get your head in the

game." She paused before saying, "The orders came down from the top in Hereford."

"Yes, ma'am. Fine, I'll go in tonight. I'm not hanging around."

"I'll have the helicopter on standby."

Hawk said, "Tell me something, Alpha One. Why can't we all go in together? Once the X-rays know something is up then the shit will hit the fan."

"It's been assessed that the risk is too great to the package, Bravo."

Of all the fucked up... In other words, the life of every other woman was considered expendable. "Did I just hear you right, Alpha One?"

"Affirmative, Bravo."

"Would you like to put me through to the bastard who made the decision, Alpha One?"

Anja's voice hardened. She didn't like the idea either, had even argued against it, but her job, like Hawk's, was to follow orders if and when they came down. "Follow the damn orders, Jake."

"Yes, ma'am."

Hawk went back to his surveillance and studied the movements of the guards. His count put at least ten of them on patrol at any one time. By his estimate there were fifty terrorists on site.

"Alpha Two, copy?"

"I'm here, Bravo," Ilse replied.

"Are you lonely, Alpha Two?"

"What the hell, Jake?" Ilse growled.

He said it again, with more emphasis. "Are you *lonely*, Alpha Two."

There was a period of silence before she said, "Switching to alternate channel."

"Roger."

After a few heartbeats, "What is it, Jake?"

"What do you have on the UAV?"

"Jake—"

"I need to know, Ilse."

"There are four Hellfires on the UAV."

"I need a direct line to the operators."

"Oh, no. Not in this lifetime, Jake. You follow the orders you have. Anything for the UAV goes through me. Understood?"

"Ilse, we can't leave the other girls there," Hawk replied. "You know, like I do, they'll kill them just as soon as they get wind of any rescue."

"Do you have a plan, Jake?"

"I'll gather them all into the culvert on the west side of the compound. I'll take them out from there."

"What if something goes wrong, Jake?"

"Then we've got Hellfires to hold them back until the Chinook arrives on station."

There was a moment of silence before Ilse said, "All right, Jake. We'll do that."

Hawk couldn't hide his relief. "Fantastic. If I wasn't all the way out here, I'd marry you."

"Don't make promises you can't keep, Jake. Out."

─────

Djibouti

"Do you have a plan, Jake?" Ilse asked.

"I'll gather them all into the culvert on the west side of the compound. I'll take them out from there."

"What if something goes wrong, Jake?"

"Then we've got Hellfires to hold them back until the Chinook arrives on station."

Ilse looked up at Anja who was standing next to her. The Talon commander nodded. Ilse said, "All right, Jake. We'll do that."

52

Hawk couldn't hide his relief. "Fantastic. If I wasn't all the way out here, I'd marry you."

"Don't make promises you can't keep, Jake. Out."

"What do you think?" Anja asked.

Ilse shrugged. "If anyone can do it, Jake can."

"I agree. Have the helicopter stand by and let the SAS commander know he may be needed at a moment's notice."

"Will do, ma'am."

"And, Ilse, not a word to anyone."

"Yes, ma'am."

Nubian Desert, Sudan

The knife grated against bone before plunging into the terrorist's heart. The man grunted in surprise but that was all because Hawk had his hand over the man's mouth. He lowered him to the ground and dragged the corpse into the dark shadows.

Back in the Tactical Operations Center, or TOC, his progress was closely monitored by ISR.

A voice filled his ear, "Bravo, you're clear to the target building."

He didn't answer, they didn't expect him to. No undue noise.

Using the shadows, he made his way towards the hut where he hoped to find Polly White. Even though he had altered the plan, he would still see that she was the priority—for the time being.

As he hit opposite it, he said into his comms, "Bravo is in position."

"Roger, Bravo. ISR feed is still the same. A single heat signature."

Checking both ways before he left cover, Hawk

crossed the space to the front door. Somehow, he managed to open the door without making a sound before slipping in. His night vision goggles cut through the dark and he saw the figure laying prone on the floor.

He crept close and kneeled beside her, putting a hand over the sleeping figure's mouth. He felt her stiffen and her hands came up to his arm. "Don't make a sound. I'm friendly."

Fingernails scratched at Hawk's hand. "Damn it, stop. I'm here to help."

The resistance stopped. Hawk said, "My name is Jake. I'm here to get you and the other girls out. I'm going to take my hand away from your mouth. If you shout, you'll get us both killed."

When he eased his hand away, she asked, "Who are you?"

She had a French accent. *Shit!* "Tell me your name."

"I am Simone Crozier, French National Gazette."

"A reporter?"

"*Oui*, yes."

"OK, sit tight." He said into his comms, "Alpha One, we've got a problem, over."

"What is it, Bravo?" Anja asked.

"The package isn't here. It's a French reporter. Simone Crozier. Over."

"Wait one, Bravo."

Hawk checked the door. He opened it a crack and looked outside. "Alpha Two, how are we looking?"

"All clear, Jake."

Anja came back. "Jake, Simone Crozier was last seen three weeks ago. Her photographer and interpreter were killed when she was taken."

"Roger that."

He went back over to Simone. "I just got confirmation about you. Now, do you know anyone named Polly White?"

"No."

"How long have you been here?"

"Three days."

"Have you had contact with any of the other girls?"

"A couple. They've been here longer than me. Some have been here four months."

"Blast."

"Wait, so you are not here for me, after all?"

"No."

"You can't leave me," she blurted out.

"I don't plan to," he replied. "Come with me and do everything I tell you."

"All right."

He led her out into the night, pausing each time they had to leave the cover of the dark shadows. Eventually they reached the culvert he had picked out to sequester the girls in. "Wait here," he said to Simone. "You should be safe."

"What are you going to do?"

"I'm going after the others."

"That is crazy," she said to him.

"That's me."

He disappeared into the darkness again. He was just about to walk around the corner of a building when Ilse said, "Jake, wait."

Her voice was hushed as though she didn't want to be overheard. Hawk stopped and tried to control his breathing. Then he heard boots crunching on the dry earth. He pressed himself against the building, back into the shadows.

The guard appeared as he walked past the corner of the building. Hawk watched him keep going.

"You're clear the other way, Jake."

He slipped around the corner and walked twenty meters to another mud hut. He tried the door. It popped open and he winced. He almost cursed out loud when he swung it open and it screeched at him. He moved quickly into the dark room to see the girl starting to move on the floor.

"Don't make a sound. I'm here to help."

Sometimes you just know that things are about to go wrong unless you react quickly, decisively. He couldn't shoot her, and he didn't want to knock her out, so, that didn't leave much. He dove forward, his fist taking her in the middle. The air rushed from her lungs thus taking away the capacity for her to scream. Then he wrapped his arms around her to keep her from running away. "Just calm down, love, and breathe. All right. I'm here to help."

"You—you hit me."

She was British.

"I'm sorry. Are you OK?"

"No, it hurt."

"Tell me your name."

"Georgina Smith."

"Where you from?" Hawk asked.

"Staffordshire."

He said into his comms. "Alpha Two. I have a Georgina Smith from Staffordshire."

"Copy, Jake. Wait one."

"How many others are with you?"

"Five came with my lot. But there are only four of us now that Polly has gone."

Hawk's blood ran cold. The package wasn't there. "What do you mean she's gone?"

"They took her away a week ago."

"Do you know where to?"

"I have no idea." She shook her head, her shaggy hair falling over her face.

Just then, Ilse's voice came over the line over comms. "Jake, I can confirm Georgina Smith from Staffordshire."

"Roger Alpha Two. Confirming Georgina Smith.

Now I have some news. The package is not on site. I repeat, the package is not on site."

"Roger, Jake, the package is not on site."

"Bravo, this is Alpha One, over."

"Bravo copies," Hawk replied.

"Confirm your last."

Hawk said, "I have a hostage on site, saying that the package left a week ago."

There was a moment of silence before Anja's voice came back, "Roger that, Jake."

"What about the others that are on site?" Hawk asked Georgina.

She said in a quiet voice, "The others are here because they want to be."

"Are you sure about that?"

"Yes," she said. "They have converted over as well. A couple of times they have beaten us for not doing what we're supposed to be doing."

Hawk thought for a moment. "Are you able to move around at night to get to the other girls?"

Georgina fidgeted and he could tell there was something wrong. "What's the matter?"

"My husband is on guard. If he comes back—"

"Wait, what?" said Hawk.

"Yes, he's on guard. We all have husbands. It was what we were brought here for."

"Shit a frigging brick."

Georgina said, "I might be able to get them though."

Hawk nodded. "Get the ones you can and bring them back here. If there are any you can't, I'll have to get them. Can you do it?"

"I think so."

"OK on your way."

Georgina left the hut and walked out into the night. Hawk said into his comms, "Alpha Two, copy?"

"Read you loud and clear, Jake."

"Moving to the next phase, over."

"Roger, looking all clear so far."

"Let's hope it stays that way," he muttered to himself.

————

"JAKE, you have someone coming your way," Ilse's voice was urgent.

Hawk moved to a position beside the door. "Copy. Give me real time updates."

"He's still coming your way. Get ready."

Hawk leaned the Bren2 against the wall and took out his knife. He waited patiently, then in the distance he could hear the footsteps growing closer. They stopped outside the door and then the door opened, its screech filling the room. The man had a flashlight and he shone it around as he entered.

The man stopped, stiffened as he realized something was wrong. Hawk moved swiftly as he clamped his left hand over the man's mouth, while the knife in his right plunged deep up through the rib cage of his back. The point pierced his heart, and Hawk pulled it out once again, then dragged it across his throat. A large slit opened, and warm blood flowed down the front of the man's chest. He died with a gurgle as Hawk lay him on the dirt floor.

"X-ray down."

Ilse's voice came across comms. "Jake, we're seeing movement around the camp. I think it's the girls. So far we have three on the move. By our calculations, there should be one more."

A few minutes later, Ilse said, "Something's wrong, Jake. They're coming your way."

"That's fine, standby, I'll deal with it."

When the three girls arrived back, they saw the body on the floor, and they all flinched at the sight of it. "What have you done?" asked one of them, her accent had her pegged as German.

"It was him or me. I chose me."

"Herr, they will kill us," her voice was high pitched from fear.

"They're not going to kill anyone," Hawk assured her. "What happened to the other girl?"

"We couldn't get to Irena. Her husband was with her."

"Well, I'm not leaving her behind," Hawk whispered harshly. "Do you girls know where the culvert is?"

"Yes," said Georgina.

"Good. I need one of you to come with me. The rest of you to go to the culvert where you'll find the French woman."

"She's coming with us?" Georgina asked.

Hawk nodded. "Yes, she's already there."

"I will show you," said Georgina.

"Fine." He looked at the remaining two girls. "Once you get to the culvert you stay there. Do not go anywhere. Do you understand?"

"Yes."

Hawk bent down and picked up an AK-47 that the man had dropped when he died. "Do either of you know how to use this?" he asked.

"I can...I think," said one of the remaining girls. This one sounded Russian.

Using his small flashlight, Hawk gave her a quick rundown. "Do not fire it unless it is really necessary, or you will bring the whole terrorist camp down upon your heads. When you get to the culvert, stay there."

They left and Hawk turned to Georgina. "Right, show me the way."

He raised his suppressed Bren2 and followed her out the door.

———

59

THE EXPLOSION ROCKED THE VILLAGE, sending an orange ball of flame into the sky. "That went to shit, really quickly," Hawk growled as bullets punched into the side of the mud building. He turned to Georgina. "Get to the culvert. I'll be there shortly."

"But what—"

"Just go, you'll be fine. They'll be worried about me. But whatever you do, don't come out."

They ran off into a darkness punctuated by bright flashes. Hawk changed out his magazine and readied himself for what was to come.

Everything had been going well until their attempt to free the last girl. A scuffle, a gunshot, and the whole village came alive.

Two shooters appeared around the corner of a building and the suppressed Bren came to life again. They fell to the hardpacked earth, dropping their weapons as they went down.

Another explosion rocked the village. This one showered Hawk with debris. "Christ, Alpha Two, have you found that frigging RPG yet?"

"We're on it, Jake. Just keep your head down."

Another explosion shook the village, this one was more powerful than the previous one as an AGM-114 Hellfire missile crashed to earth at almost 1,000 MPH.

"Target down hard, Jake."

Hawk peered around the corner of the building where he hid. Four terrorists were running in his direction. He reached to his webbing, or Personal Load Carrying Equipment as it was known, for a grenade. He pulled the pin and threw it around the corner in front of the rapidly advancing enemy.

He waited, counting off seconds in his head before a loud CRUMP! could be heard as the anti-personnel weapon detonated.

Hawk came out of cover, his weapon raised. Three of

the four terrorists were down, the last staggering around, his clothes torn to shreds. The Brit fired his Bren and the killer fell beside his friends.

"How far out is that helicopter, Alpha Two?" Hawk asked.

"They're saying ten mikes, Jake. They're having trouble with sand in something. If they don't get it out, then the thing will crash."

A wave of frustration came over Hawk but there was no time to vent it. "What about the SAS team?"

"Same."

"Roger that."

"Jake, you've got two X-rays coming up on your six." This was Karl.

Hawk turned just as the two Sudanese terrorists appeared. Both were carrying AK-47s. The Brit fired, and first one, then the other, fell.

He started walking to his right where a narrow alley went between two mud huts, disappearing just as a handful of terrorists appeared.

Hawk said, "Do you have a track on those two girls?"

"They're almost there, Jake. But you have bigger issues to worry about. In a matter of moments, your position will be surrounded by X-rays looking for you."

"Find me a path through."

"There is none. You'll have to go inside the hut next—too late. There is an X-ray coming at you from the front. You should see him...now."

The terrorist appeared and Hawk put him down before the shooter realized what was happening.

Suddenly Hawk noticed multiple orange glows appearing above the roofs of the buildings in the village. "What's with the fires?" he asked Ilse.

"It looks like they're using them for light."

"There goes the advantage," the Brit growled. "Watch my six, Alpha, I'm headed for the girls."

Hawk pushed forward in the direction of the culvert. He emerged from an alley and was faced with a handful of shooters and a technical with a fifty-caliber machine gun attached to it.

Instinctively, the Brit brought his Bren up and opened fire. Two X-rays dropped before the others reacted and began firing back at him, their heightened awareness quickening their response time.

Hawk ducked behind a mudbrick wall opposite just as bullets hammered into it. A short time later, the cracks of the lighter weapons was joined by the chug-chug of the Fifty.

Suddenly, all around Hawk, the wall started to disappear in large chunks. He rose to fire at the technical but more gunfire from the 50-caliber forced him back down. He slid along the wall as small mud bricks exploded behind him. Once more, he rose, dropped the laser sight on the shooter behind the 50 caliber and then fired two shots into his chest.

The heavy caliber machine gun went silent, but there were still two more shooters firing in this direction. Hawk came up and felt the tug of a bullet at his sleeve, but he ignored it and then fired it nearest to the two shooters. The man cried out and fell backwards as a 5.56 millimeter round hammered into his chest.

Another loud roar filled the air as a second technical appeared from behind one of the houses. It, too, supported a fifty-caliber machine gun which started firing instantly when the technical stopped.

Hawk said into his comms, "I could do with the hand of God about now."

"Hang on," Ilse said. "We'll have something on the way in a moment."

"Just take your time. I've got all night," Hawk growled as more of the wall disappeared around him.

"Jake, the UAV operators are refusing to fire unless you give your permission. They're saying danger close."

"Patch me through."

"The link is up, Jake. Callsign is Unicorn One."

"Unicorn one. This is Alpha One, over."

"Roger Alpha One. This is Unicorn One, reading you loud and clear."

"Unicorn One, I need you to put a lance through that frigging technical, over."

"Copy, Alpha One. You're asking for fire support, danger close? Over."

"Just get the bastard in here before I lose all my cover."

The operator's calm voice came back over the comms. "Roger, Alpha one. Sit tight, on its way."

What was in fact only a second seemed like minutes as their heavy 50-caliber machine gun blew most of Hawk's cover away around him. Suddenly it sounded like a freight train coming out of the sky, followed by the explosion as the technical and those around it disappeared in an orange ball of flame.

Not waiting, Hawk came to his feet and started to push forward once more. Towards the culvert an X-ray appeared on his left and he swiveled in his hips, dropping the terrorist with a couple of well-placed shots.

Another shooter appeared and the Brit lined his weapon up to fire. He squeezed the trigger, but nothing happened. He let go of the Bren, which fell until its strap snapped taut. Hawk grabbed at his SIG P226 and brought it up, firing three times, making sure the shooter went down.

Bullets kicked up dirt at Hawk's feet. He spun and dropped to a knee, firing at another X-ray. The killer's right leg kicked out from beneath him and with a yelp of pain he fell into a heap.

Hawk walked towards him, firing the SIG as he went. Bullet strikes could be seen hitting the fallen shooter, as he jerked under each impact. The handgun fell silent as the magazine ran dry. Hawk dropped it out, changed in the fresh one before holstering it, and then doing the same with his Bren2.

More X-rays appeared. Something sailed through the air and landed near Hawk with a dull thud. He caught a glance of the grenade and swore, "You have got to be fucking kidding me."

The small antipersonnel device exploded, violently thrusting Hawk off his feet, as though he'd been shoved by a giant hand. He hit the hard-packed earth solidly, the air gushing from his body. Desperately trying to reinflate his lungs by sucking great gulps, he managed to moan, "Unicorn One. I need another Hellfire now."

"What target, Alpha One?"

"Danger close," he groaned.

"On its way."

———

Djibouti

"He can't keep this up for much longer," Ilse said looking at Anja, her face a mask of fear.

"He has to," the Talon commander replied coolly. "He has no other choice."

They both held their breath when they saw the explosion and Hawk thrown from his feet by the blast. They heard his voice come over the radio as he ordered another strike. He was alive at least, but he didn't sound good.

The Hellfire hit with a bright flash, and it looked as though most of the attackers fell. Then they heard Hawk say, "Now the other one."

Ilse glanced at Anja. If the last Hellfire was launched Hawk would have no more backup until the helicopter or SAS arrived.

The console operator could be heard to say, "Bravo One, repeat your last."

He knew what the two women were thinking.

"Find a target and put the last bloody Hellfire on it," Hawk growled.

"That is our last Hellfire, Bravo One."

"I can count."

Anja had heard enough. "Jake, this is Anja. If you expend the last Hellfire, then you have nothing until backup arrives. That is still five minutes out."

"I won't need backup if you don't use it," he shot back at them.

Anja thought about it some more before saying, "Ilse, do it."

"Unicorn One, this is Alpha Two. Cleared hot."

"Roger, ma'am."

"I just hope he knows what he's doing."

"So do I," whispered Anja to herself.

———

Nubian Desert, Sudan

Hawk, however, had a plan. He'd managed to find some cover, and he spent time removing the remaining grenades from his webbing, and then reloaded the Bren2 with a full magazine, taking the suppressor off. Then he waited.

When the final Hellfire hit, the ground shook. Hawk then threw his grenades, waiting for them to explode. Once they had erupted, he emptied the magazine like some crazed wild man firing at nothing. He reloaded quickly.

The noise he created made it seem that the village was being attacked by a large force which is exactly what he wanted.

Hawk came to his feet as the echoes of the firing died

away. A single terrorist appeared, running across his path, not looking, just running. The Brit let him go.

Taking a few steps forward, Hawk winced. He could feel the blood from a cut on his left arm. He looked at it in the firelight of a burning technical. He shrugged; a few stitches would close it. "Alpha Two, what do you see?"

"Wait one, Bravo."

Another terrorist appeared. This one stopped, stared at Hawk, and scrambled to get his AK around to shoot at the Brit. The Bren came up and rattled to life. The terrorist was hit in the chest and dead before he sprawled on the ground.

"Are you there, Jake?"

As Hawk looked around the village, he said, "I'm here."

"It looks like the terrorists are bugging out. Whatever it is you intended to do, it looked like it worked."

"Roger that. How far out is helicopter?"

"I've just been told a couple of minutes," Ilse responded.

"Better late than never, I guess."

CHAPTER SIX

Djibouti

GEORGINA LOOKED TIRED, but she was the one most likely to give them the answers they needed. Everyone had been checked over when they arrived back, including Hawk. Now, Hawk and Anja were sitting in a small room where they could question Georgina and record the conversation.

"Do you have any idea where they might have taken her?" Anja asked again for the tenth time.

Georgina shook her head again. "No, no, I can't think of anything."

Hawk said, "There was no mention of transport or anything like that?"

The girl sat there in silence; her eyes half closed. She concentrated trying to think of anything, even a scrap of information that may have seemed insignificant. She started to shake her head slowly and then stopped. "Wait. There was something."

"What?" Anja asked.

"A name."

"Can you remember it?"

"Ivan Franko," she replied hesitantly. "Yes, that's it. Ivan Franko."

"Was there anything else?"

Georgina shook her head. "No, nothing else. I do hope I've helped. Polly was so nice. She was good to all of us. Please find her."

Hawk nodded. "We will do our best."

Anja looked at her. "Get some rest. In a day or so, you'll be heading home."

The girl gave them a wan smile. "Home. I almost gave up on thinking I'd ever see it again. Thank you for freeing us."

After she was taken away, Hawk and Anja joined Ilse and Karl. "How is she doing?" the Intel analyst asked.

Anja said, "It'll take her a while to get over it, but she seems strong enough. What did we learn from our French woman?"

"Not a lot," Karl replied. "She was kept away from the rest of them. Had no interaction at all. Did you get anything?"

"A name," said Hawk. "Ivan Franko. Do you want to chase it down for us?"

Karl nodded. "Chasing things down is what I do these days."

He walked away muttering to himself, off to do his thing, leaving the other three standing there staring at each other. "What do we do now?" asked Hawk.

"We wait," replied Anja. "What happened with the girls' tattoos?"

"I waved our magic wand over them before we boarded the helicopter," Hawk informed her.

Ilse said, "It seemed to work well."

"All right. Jake, get some rest. You look about out on your feet."

"Yes, ma'am."

Anja left them and Ilse asked Hawk, "How are you feeling?"

"Like I was run over by a lorry," he told her truthfully.

"You gave us a moment or two there."

"You? I gave me some, too."

"What did the doctor say?"

Hawk shrugged. "Just told me to rest up. Give my arm a chance to heal."

"Then do just that. I'll be around to check on you later."

Hawk grinned at her. "Yes, mother."

———

Somewhere in Europe

Enjoying a casual dinner of veal cordon bleu, Viktor Medvedev looked across at his dining companion. He picked up his wine glass half-filled from the bottle of Italian red wine beside him and slurped noisily. "How many do you need, Hakim?"

Hakim Anwar, the man at the top of Talon's current shit list. Anwar stared at the man opposite him contemplating a number. Medvedev was former Russian FSB. In his mid-forties with black hair, dyed that way to disguise the sea of gray coming through. Anwar, on the other hand, was a suave man still in his late thirties who dressed well.

"I'm thinking maybe five."

Medvedev nodded, putting down his glass and steepling his fingers in a gesture of contemplation. "I think I can do that. Any kind in particular?"

The sex trafficker shrugged. "Maybe African. As black as you can get them. I have several clients who love that kind of thing."

"I don't see a problem with that."

Anwar forked a piece of schnitzel into his mouth. He

chewed for a bit, swallowed, and then asked Medvedev, "I heard you had some troubles recently."

The Medusa boss looked up. "Nothing I can't handle. However, I'm interested in a mutual friend who has suddenly left your employ."

"You heard about that?"

"I hear a lot of things. I received news earlier today that mercenaries raided a training camp of the North African Freedom Fighters in Sudan. I assume they were after a certain young woman who, luckily, happened to be shifted over a week ago. Mustafa Osman sent her to a contact in Saudi Arabia. Her destination is an auction in Riyadh where she will be sold with a certain select few. It promises to be a grand evening."

"I see."

"I'm wondering how they got the information about Osman's camp but then I guess we both already know that."

"Is there something I can help you with?" Anwar asked, trying to change the subject.

Medvedev gave a slight nod. "There might well be."

"Then ask."

"Consider this a formal invitation to the auction. I will be there of course plus a few European buyers."

"I still don't get what you want from me."

"I want you there as bait."

Anwar snorted. "You can't be serious."

Medvedev said nothing.

"You are?"

"Consider this as something mutually beneficial for us both; you do this for me and I will waive the fee for your recent order. And overlook the fact that your man seems to be assisting our mutual enemies."

"You can't hold me responsible for what I have no control over," Anwar protested, sitting up straight and wiping his mouth with his napkin.

"You will be there, Hakim. Or you will never do business with me again. And you know what that means."

"These are the same people who killed Charlotte Allard."

Medvedev let the comment go. After all, he was the one responsible for her demise.

Anwar put his knife and fork down. "I, too, have heard about these people, Viktor. It seems that you know one of them very well indeed. Anja Meyer, formerly of German intelligence."

What he said was true. He and Anja had history. Brutal history in which he'd shot her, but the bitch refused to die. "You will be there, Anwar. You will be there."

"Tell me, Viktor, was it your people in Antwerp? Were they the ones who caused chaos on the streets?"

Medvedev nodded. "They were."

"Why didn't you warn me? I could have taken steps."

"Goodbye, Hakim. I will see you in Riyadh. The itinerary will be forwarded to you."

Shocked at being dismissed in such a way, Anwar glared at Medvedev, screwing his napkin up into a ball, and threw it onto his half-eaten meal. Then, without a word, he stood up and left.

Anwar was replaced in the chair by Ilya Noskov. "Is he going to be trouble?"

Medvedev shook his head. "I do not think so. Are the preparations being made?"

"Yes. Our friend in Riyadh has been most accommodating."

"Then it is a wait and see situation."

"I wanted to ask about the tattoos," Noskov said.

"What about them?"

"I don't see the point of them."

"They help me find runaways."

"They are a waste of time. Especially now that the

mercenaries have something to counteract and disable the isotope."

"How do you know this?"

"The ones on the girls in Sudan were disabled after the village was hit."

"You checked?"

"Yes, I thought I might be able to use it to get a location on the ones responsible."

Medvedev stared at Noskov. He wasn't used to men standing up to him like this. The former colonel was definitely not Leonid. He nodded. "Fine. Have them stopped. Anything else?"

"No."

"Then we shall prepare to leave for Riyadh."

————

Djibouti

"Any luck with Ivan Franko?" Anja asked Karl who was almost buried in his screen.

"Not the one we want," he replied, not looking up. "I never knew there were so many Ivan Frankos in the world."

"Any of them stand out?"

"Three. One in Belarus, another in Russia, and a third in Ukraine."

"The one in Russia, what does he do?" Anja asked.

"Car thief."

"Ukraine?"

"Wife beater."

"Shit. What about Bel—"

"Another thief."

"So, nothing hard core?"

"No."

"There has to be something we're missing."

Karl said, finally looking at his boss. "I agree."

"Widen the search parameters. People, anagrams, towns, it must be code for something."

"Yes, ma'am."

Hawk entered the ops center. "Any luck?"

Anja shook her head. "Nothing yet."

Hawk sighed. "The longer this takes, the more likely Polly White will be lost forever in the darkness."

"I realize that, Jake, but there's only so much we can do." Her tone told him that she knew what was at stake.

"Tell me this, then. Osman had her and it is assumed he was going to make an example out of her. But then he sends her off. Why?"

"That is a good question."

"Money," Karl said, breaking in.

They turned and looked at him. "You mean he sold her?" Hawk asked.

"Or is intending to."

"But why?"

"Money to buy arms. A British politician's daughter will garner a good price."

"He'll need an auction with high-priced buyers," Anja said. "And below the radar transport. Nothing around facial recognition?"

"Bastard," Karl growled. "I can't believe I didn't think of it until now."

Anja stared at him. "Think of what?"

"Ivan Franko. You said they would need off the radar travel. What kind of travel is actually off the radar? Well, it's not actually off the radar, but it's close to it."

Hawk nodded. "You're talking about a ship."

"Yes, I am."

Karl's fingers danced across the keyboard of his computer. "Ivan Franco isn't a bloody name. Well, it is a name. But it's a ship, not a person."

"It's a good way of getting someone into a country

undetected," Hawk agreed. "Pay the right people and no one sees anything."

"And there it is," Karl said as he hit the key and a picture of a large container ship appeared on the screen.

"Do we know where it is?" Anja asked.

"We will in a moment," Karl assured her.

Once more, his fingers danced across the keyboard as he entered different bits of code and did his search. It wasn't long before the information he requested flashed up onto the screen. "According to this, the ship is now docked in Jeddah, Saudi Arabia."

"Then we need to get a look on that ship."

"Do you think she will still be there?" Hawk asked.

"What do you suggest, Jake?"

"I would look at Riyadh. If anybody is going to do any selling in that country, that's where it's going to be. That's where all the money is."

Anja nodded. "Then Riyadh is where we'll go."

CHAPTER SEVEN

Riyadh, Saudi Arabia

THE BRITISH EMBASSY in Riyadh was more like a squat five-star hotel, complete with four floors, two swimming pools, lush gardens, and a high reinforced steel fence. It had been opened all of twelve months, a gift from the House of Saud.

When the team arrived, they were mightily impressed. Originally, they had thought that they would be put up at an MI6 safe house somewhere within the city, but certain parties in the government intervened, and the embassy was to become their home.

Their MI6 liaison officer was a man named Paul Grayson. In his forties, he'd been stationed in the city for the past two years. His orders were to provide the team with all the help they required, and in doing so, set them up in one of the embassy's operations rooms.

"If there is anything you need, let me know," he said to Anja. "My people are here to help."

"We saw some smoke on the way in," Anja replied. "What was that all about?"

"There's a little bit of civil unrest happening I'm

afraid. Happens every now and then. They start out protesting one thing, the radical factions infiltrate, and before you know it you have a full-on bloody riot on your hands."

"What is the chatter?" Ilse asked.

Grayson stared at her in silence.

"I am the team's intelligence officer. If there is something that could affect the operation, I need to know."

The MI6 man nodded. "Both us and the Americans have received intel that the Houthis may have something planned within the next forty-eight to seventy-two hours."

"What kind of something?" Anja asked.

"We're not sure. But they do have their supporters amongst the population. Those that are fed up with the current rule."

"That's all we need."

"Yes, it would be inconvenient to say the least." He sighed. "Well, like I said, if you need anything."

"Thank you."

"My pleasure."

Hawk looked around the room at all the screens and electronic equipment. "I wonder just how secure this room actually is."

"It is now," one of the techs said. "Apparently when it was taken over the sweepers found thousands of bugs and a good deal of hidden cameras."

Hawk chuckled. "I bet the ambassador was pleased that they found all of those before he got up to any mischief."

The tech gave him a puzzled look. "Sir?"

"Never mind."

The Brit looked at Ilse and shook his head. She grinned but remained silent.

One of the techs stood up from where they were stationed and approached Ilse. She was a young woman, perhaps mid-twenties. "Ma'am, I heard you say you were the intel officer?"

Ilse nodded. "That's right."

"My name is Patience. I'm one of the techs assigned to assist."

Ilse smiled warmly. "Pleased to meet you. Call me Ilse. This lunatic here is Jake. He's our field agent."

She smiled nervously at Hawk who nodded back. "Don't listen to her. I'm much worse."

Patience's brows shot up. "You're British."

Hawk grinned. "And about the only sane one amongst them."

Ilse rolled her eyes. "Oh, please. What was it, Patience?"

"I was doing a search using the parameters you wanted, and I think I've come up with a couple of things."

"Show me."

Hawk joined them at the console where Patience linked her computer to a larger screen. "I managed to get this off some security footage. If you take a close look, I think it might be Polly White."

As they watched the screen, they saw someone being escorted off the container ship *Ivan Franko*. An armed men stood either side of her as they walked down the gangplank. When they hit the bottom of the gangplank, the prisoner looked up and Patience stopped the feed. "Is that her?"

Ilse nodded. "It certainly looks like her. Who are those people with her?"

"I'm working on facial recognition. I am hoping to have something soon."

"Do we know where they took her?" Hawk asked.

"I'm working on that, too. I'm hopeful that once we can ID one of the two with her then we might be able to get a location."

As they watched further, they saw the men put Polly

White into a black SUV, and then they themselves climbed in. Seconds later, they left the dock.

"I'll let Anja know," Ilse said. "She'll be eager to hear the news."

After she had left, Hawk asked Patience, "Is the ship still in port?"

"I'll check."

After a couple of moments and some key tapping, she looked up and said, "Yes."

"Great. While you're still figuring things out, I'm going to have someone do some old-fashioned investigating."

"Be careful, Jake. It is a whole different world out there."

Hawk gave her a broad grin. "It'll be fine."

Jeddah, Saudi Arabia

"It won't be fucking fine," Jocko Jackson growled into the cell he held up to his ear. "This isn't some fucking backwater shitter, Jake. It's Saudi Arabia. They're a law unto themselves here. I only think about doing something wrong and they'll have me banged up for twenty years. I should have hung up when you asked if I was still in Jeddah."

Hawk waited for his friend to finish. "Are you done, Jocko?"

Jackson remained silent.

"Good. All I need you to do is get on the ship and have a word to the captain."

Jackson closed his brown eyes, then ran a hand through his dark hair. He could feel the frustration building inside at what was being asked of him. "No, Jake. I'm not fucking doing it."

"I didn't want to do this, Jocko, but you owe me. A young lady's life is at stake here."

"Bloody hell, Jake. What do you want me to do?" His breath hissed out in a frustrated sigh.

Hawk ran through the predicament he was in, all the while Jackson listened quietly. When he was done Jocko sighed. "If I do this, Jake, we're all square."

"As all four sides, Jocko. As all four sides."

"I hope I'm getting fucking paid for this. Am I?"

"How does five thousand sound?"

Jackson snorted. "Like bloody shit Jake. Not worth getting out of bed for five grand. Double it and I'll think about it."

"Fine," replied Hawk. "I'll see that you get it."

"One more thing," said Jackson. "What happens if things go wrong, and I get banged up?"

"I'll do what I can for you. But if something does go wrong, these people are armed, Jocko, I can't imagine you'll get banged up."

"Thanks a lot, *mate*."

The call disconnected and Jackson sat there for a moment looking at the cell. The former SAS man turned security guard had been in Saudi Arabia for the last four years. The security business paid well and he quite enjoyed it. But today was one of those days where he wished he was in another country far away. He shook his head. "Fucking Jake."

He knew for sure that if he got caught doing something illegal, he was as good as gone. But Jake pulling him out of a nest of terrorists when he was wounded back in 2014 was something he just didn't ignore.

Their troop had been acting on intelligence about a village in Afghanistan where insurgents were hiding out. The intel also had the insurgent leader, Babak Julid, supposedly onsite.

They had been inserted by two Black Hawks around a

mile from the village. From there they had gone in on foot. Hawk had been in charge of one of the teams. The idea was to approach the target building from two different directions.

But somehow the insurgents had gotten wind of what was planned and been prepared for them. Not long after they entered the village, one of the teams was hit. And hit hard. That was the team that Jackson was in.

Three men went down in the first salvo of the ambush as the night lit up with tracer rounds. Two were dead and Jackson was hit hard. He lay trapped in the open.

The first hint of trouble was the gunfire that reached out across the village to Hawk's team. Then came the urgent radio call requesting help.

Hawk, being Hawk, led his team into the teeth of battle. The insurgents hadn't been aware that the SAS had split into two groups and Hawk had hit them from behind. Even though they were taken by surprise, the insurgents still put up stiff resistance. They smelled blood and victory was within their grasp.

Then he heard the call that someone had seen one of the three downed soldiers moving. He also knew that if the insurgents spotted the man, they would target him immediately and kill him.

Without any thought for his own safety, Hawk located the wounded man, went out into the open and brought him in. Then he called in an airstrike while the team medic worked on Jackson, trying to save his life.

Jackson rubbed at the scars on the side of his chest where the bullets had missed his body armor. If it hadn't been for Hawk, he would be dead.

"Fuck it, Jake."

GETTING onto the ship hadn't been easy, but for a man with Jackson's skillset it wasn't impossible. First there were the checkpoints he had to avoid, the armed guards as well, then the cameras. He'd negated them by coming aboard from the sea side of the *Ivan Franko*.

Once aboard he avoided all roving guards and made his way to the superstructure at the stern of the ship.

Finally inside, Jackson worked his way down the length of a narrow corridor towards the captain's cabin. Silently he let himself in to find the man fast asleep. The cabin smelled of stale sweat and alcohol.

Clamping his hand over the captain's mouth, he placed the point of the knife against the exposed flesh of the rapidly waking man's throat. "Try anything and I'll open you from ear to fucking ear," Jackson whispered harshly.

The captain grunted from behind the hand.

"You brought a girl into the country, yes?"

"Hmpf."

"I'll take that as a yes. Who took her?"

The man said something, but it was incoherent because of the hand. "I'm going to move my hand. You try to call out, and I'll gut you like a fish."

Jackson removed his hand and asked the question again. "Adnan Kamal," the captain replied. "It was he who came."

"Who is Adnan Kamal?"

"He works for Dasan Ansari."

The name was well-known. Dasan Ansari was a rich man and it was said most of his money was procured by other than legal means.

"Why is he taking her?"

"To—to sell. The money is for Mustafa Osman. Ansari helps fund their efforts."

Happy with the answers, Jackson said, "Now, what do I do with you?"

"Please, do not kill me. I can tell no one. If I do, I am a dead man anyway."

The captain spoke with genuine fear, and besides, Jackson didn't want to kill him if he didn't have to. Instead, he hit him and left him there knocked out cold.

Riyadh, Saudi Arabia

"I have a name for you, Jake," Jocko said to Hawk. "Actually it's two names. Dasan Ansari and Adnan Kamal."

Hawk smiled. "Great show, old son. Although it seems to me I should know this Ansari blighter."

"You should. He's one of the richest tossers in Riyadh. Most of it come by illegally. A lot of people have died for that wealth."

"Then why hasn't he been shut down yet?"

"Because he is some distant stepson to a cousin of a brother of a royal family member, take your pick."

Hawk knew how that went. There were some 15,000 members of the royal family in Saudi Arabia. 4000 or so of them were princes. If he was in any way connected, he would have all the protection in the world. This was not going to be easy.

"Thanks, Jocko. You're a bloody corker, mate."

"We're square, Jake. If you have any more trouble, find someone else."

"If I have any more trouble, Jocko, I'll probably never be seen again."

The call disconnected and Hawk punched in the number for Ilse. "What is it, Jake?"

"Did I disturb your breakfast?"

"At five-thirty in the morning?"

Hawk looked at his watch. "Sorry, but I have news. My man came through. Do you want me to call the boss?"

"I'll do that, Jake. She'll probably appreciate it more if it comes from me."

"Roger that."

"I'll see you in the ops room in thirty minutes."

"You might want to wake the techs up as well. This is going to be big."

"I'm dreading it already."

ANJA SAT UP IN BED, the thin sheet falling away from her torso, exposing her nakedness and the accumulation of scars. It was just too hot to sleep in anything.

She reached over to the angrily buzzing cell phone and put it up to her ear. "What is it?"

"Jake has something for us," Ilse said. "He wants us to gather in the operations room."

Anja sighed. "I'll be there shortly."

She dropped back down on the bed, staring at the ceiling in contemplation. She ran her delicate fingers over the scars on her chest, each one a reminder of the man that she hated more than anything in the world.

Still plagued by nightmares, Anja often found herself waking through the night, drenched in sweat. She also knew that nothing would change on that score until she stopped the man responsible and put him in the ground. It was the only possible solution; jail would never be enough.

Anja climbed out of bed and slipped into a pair of shorts and a T-shirt. She slipped her handgun in the back of the pair of her pants and then picked her cell phone up from the side table. For some reason, she had the feeling it was going to be a long day.

83

HAWK GRINNED at Anja and couldn't help himself. "Are you going on holiday to the beach, ma'am?"

Anja's eyes narrowed. "Get on with it, Jake."

"I actually think you should wear something like that more often. It shows off your legs."

"I've not had coffee yet, Jacob, and you are coming at me with lines like that. Please give me one good reason why I should not shoot you now and go back to bed."

"Dasan Ansari."

Anja's expression changed. "I'm starting to like your foreplay, Mister Hawk. Tell me more."

The Brit grinned. "My friend managed to get onto the Ivan Franco. He had a little chat to the captain and found out from him that the people who picked up Polly White work for Ansari."

"This is not good," Patience said in a troubled voice. "The man is almost untouchable."

Hawk smirked and said, "I like that word almost. It's the difference between not touchable and me being able to reach out and just tap him on the shoulder. It becomes a challenge."

"No, almost untouchable means untouchable. You cannot get near him."

Ilse saw the glint in Hawk's eye then said to Patience in a despairing voice, "Why did you have to say that?"

Anja looked at Ilse. "I want everything we can gather on Ansari. Right down to his security detail."

"Yes, ma'am."

"Check the name, Adnan Kamal. He is one of the guys who picked Polly up from the ship," Hawk said.

Ilse nodded and turned away.

Next, Anja said to Karl, "I want you to scan every damn security camera in this city. I want to know who the people are that are coming in and going out. Everything. If Ansari is having an auction, shy of a guest list, I want to know who is going to be there."

"I will see to it."

Lastly, she said to Patience, "You have the important job. I want you to find out where and when the auction will take place. It has to be soon."

"Yes, ma'am."

"What do you want me to do?" Hawk piped up from beside her.

"Help Ilse. If you can locate Adnan Kamal then you might be able to question him."

"If I question him, I'm not going to be able to let him go," Hawk said.

"Understood."

———

"HAVE you found out the location of the auction?" Hawk asked Patience as she joined them.

She shook her head. "Not yet, but I can tell you where it's most likely going to be."

"I'm all ears."

She brought up a picture of a skyscraper on the big screen. Hawk took one look at it and his heart sank. "It better not be there," he said. "It looks to be all of one hundred floors bloody high."

"It's called The Sands," Patience replied. "And it's only eighty floors."

Ilse stared at Patience. "Did you say it was called The Sands?"

"That's right."

"Shit," she sighed.

Hawk looked to Ilse, waiting for her to expound. "What seems to be the problem?"

"It could be nothing but..."

"Don't tell me, every person we've been tracking coming into the country in the past few days, is staying there?"

85

"Only the Russian, the one from Belarus, the Italian, the German. Should I go on?"

Hawk shook his head. "Don't bother, I get the picture. We're screwed."

An alarm began beeping on the laptop that Ilse was working on. She looked at the screen and stared at the face of the man who'd appeared. "Look who's just come into the country."

"Hakim Anwar," Hawk said. "Just the man we're after."

"And the man we're going to have to let go," Ilse said. "The target is Polly White."

The alarm sounded again and this time another face appeared. Ilse gasped while Hawk stared at the familiar face. The intelligence officer said, "Good Lord, it's him."

"It's a fucking trap," Hulk growled. "Patience, you'd better get the boss."

————

"IT'S A BLOODY TRAP. I tell you," Hawk stated for the third time. "Why else would that bastard stick his head above ground? He knows we're here and he's using himself and Anwar as bait."

Anja nodded. "That well may be true, but we're still going ahead with the operation. Nothing has changed, Polly White is still the mission."

Hawk couldn't believe what he was hearing. "Nothing has changed? What do you mean nothing has changed? Everything has bloody changed."

"Jake—"

"No," Hawk growled, rubbing at his head and pacing back and forth near the desk. As he returned to stand beside her, pointing a finger at her, he demanded, "How much of this is for the mission and how much is personal?"

Anja's eyes narrowed as she glared at the Brit.

"Damn it, Jake, you're out of line," Ilse snapped.

"Let him go, Ilse," Anja said in a low voice. "Every person on this team has a right to be heard. Just be careful, Mister Hawk, I will only take so much."

Hawk nodded. He had something to say, and he meant to say it. "Listen, I know you want this guy, we all do. But this is a trap. Any one from a mile away can see it. If we go in there, they'll see us coming and pick us off. We won't stand a chance."

"What if they don't see us coming?"

Hawk looked at her as though she were crazy. "What?"

She surprised him by smiling.

The Brit shook his head. "I'm not going to like this, am I?"

Anja shrugged. "Oh, I don't know. I kind of think that something this crazy might be right up your alley."

He glanced at Ilse. "This is going to hurt."

The Talon commander said, "Listen and I'll tell you how much."

When she was finished, Hawk didn't know whether to laugh or cry. "You can't be serious."

"I'm very serious."

"That's going to take a lot of pulling together."

"Agreed. That's why we need to lock down the date of the auction so we know how much time we have to prepare."

It was Patience that said, "It would have to be within the next 24 to 48 hours, wouldn't you think? Why would he risk being on the ground or in one place for longer than that?"

Concurring, Anja nodded as she looked at her team. "Find out. And find out fast."

As they started to turn away, the Talon commander said, "Stay behind please, Jake."

She waited until everybody was gone before she said,

"I don't mind being questioned, Jake. Even made aware of a way things can be done differently. But I won't have you questioning me in front of the whole team. You are undermining my authority. If there is something you need to get off your chest, then we do it in private. Otherwise, you bite your tongue. Is that understood?"

"I apologize, boss. I could have handled it a little bit differently. But now we're on our own. Can you honestly say that this isn't personal?"

"Although your concerns are founded, Jake, I've already lost a team once, I will not do anything to jeopardize this one."

"Yes, ma'am, that's all I ask."

"What do you think of the plan?"

He grinned at her. "It's fucking crazy."

Anja smiled herself. "Yes, I thought so."

———

"I'VE TRACKED DOWN OUR DRIVER," Patience said to Ilse and Hawk. "You're not going to like it, though."

Hawk said. "It seems to be the day for it, so hit me with it."

"He is Saudi Mabahith."

"Good grief, he's secret police."

Patient nodded. "Yes, which explains why it's taken so long to find him."

"Then he should know about the auction, yes?" Ilse asked.

"More than likely, yes. He most likely will have some security on the ground as well."

Hawk chuckled. "This just keeps getting better and better. I'm starting to think I might just shoot myself now."

Ilse patted him on the back. "You love it, Jake. This is what you live for. It keeps you alive."

He gave her a wry smile. "Until it doesn't."

"Were you able to source the things that we needed?" Ilse asked Patience.

"Yes, everything should be in position by the time you need it."

"Great."

"What are you going to do, Jake?" Ilse asked.

"I'm going to ask Kamal nicely if he'll tell me what I want to know."

"Don't get caught."

"I wouldn't dream of it." He stared at Patience. "Now, where is he?"

CHAPTER EIGHT

Riyadh, Saudi Arabia

TAKING down a member of the Saudi secret police was a bad idea at the best of times. Doing it in broad daylight was just damn crazy, and Hawk ran through every scenario in his head once more. Coming up with a less than forty percent chance that it would go off without a hitch. Actually, it was closer to ten percent.

For two hours, Hawk tailed Kamal as he went from place to place. It took a while, but the Brit finally worked out what he was up to. The man was calling into illegal gambling venues and collecting payment.

A strict Islamic country, Saudi Arabia had laws against gambling. Anyone caught faced serious consequences.

The front this time was an electronics store. Hawk watched and waited for Kamal to enter, before climbing from the vehicle he was in. He could feel the P226 nestled at the base of his spine as he crossed the street.

Almost as soon as he entered, a man came up to him. "Can I help you, sir?"

Hawk nodded. "I'm looking for a new cell phone."

The man raised his eyebrows. "You are British."

"Do I get a discount for that?"

While the salesman was talking to him, Hawk's eyes floated around the shop, discerning at least two security cameras. He pointed at one of them. "I wouldn't have thought you would need one of those in here. I heard that Saudi Arabia was a law-abiding country."

The salesman smiled. "Between you and me, sir, they are just for show, they do not work. We do not have robberies here."

The tone of Hawk's voice changed. "That's good to know."

Being the only one in the store made his next job that much easier. His right fist shot out and clipped the salesman under the jaw. Teeth clicked together solidly, and the man's eyes rolled back into his head. He fell to the ground at Hawk's feet, out cold.

Reaching down, Hawk grabbed the man by his suit collar. He dragged him across the floor and tucked him in behind the sales counter. After which he hurried back across to the door, locked it, and then reversed the sign to make sure it said closed.

Then he went out the back.

When he walked through the rear door, he found himself in a hallway with another door at the far end. The closer he got to it, the louder the voices beyond it became. He eased the door open, his hand tucked behind his back, resting on the butt of the P226.

Past the entrance was a larger room. One filled with people and gambling tables. Men were standing all around them, money going from hands onto tables, chips being passed across the felt tops.

This is going to be interesting.

He did a quick scan of the room and picked out two bodyguards, one in each corner. Hawk closed the door behind him, and immediately, people started looking in his direction. In a way he did look out of place.

A man in a suit with a bow tie and a red carnation in his pocket walked over to Hawk and said, "You do not belong here, sir."

Hawk looked him up and down and asked, "Who the fuck are you?"

"I am Ahmed, sir."

The Talon operator took a gamble. "Were you working here last night?"

Ahmed shook his head. "No, sir."

"Well, I was here last night. I want to see your boss."

"I am afraid he is quite busy, sir."

By this time, the two security guards had joined them. The bigger of the two stared arrogantly at Hawk and said, "Is there a problem?"

"There is no problem. The man was just leaving."

"The fuck I was. I want to see your boss and I mean now."

"Sir, if you do not leave, I'm afraid—"

"What are you going to do? Call the fucking police?"

Ahmed indicated to the two men beside him. "These gentlemen will escort you out. Good day, sir."

"Touch me and I'll put you in the *fucking hospital*!" he finished with a shout.

"Sir—"

"Is there a problem here?"

Hawk looked around to see Kamal standing beside the owner. "Not anymore there isn't."

The P226 came out from behind Hawk's back and snapped up into line with the first security man. He squeezed the trigger, and the flat report of the silenced weapon was heard by those in the room.

The security guard dropped like a stone onto the red and black carpet, his blood starting to soak through the coarse fibers. Hawk changed his aim and shot the second security guard in the chest twice. The man jerked violently before staggering backward and falling into a sitting position as blood began covering the white shirt beneath his black jacket.

Once more, the weapon moved, this time to cover Kamal. "Don't move, mate, I'd hate to ruin your day."

Kamal froze, his eyes narrowing. "Do you realize what you are doing?"

Hawk grinned. "I know, I know. This is where you tell me that I'm making a huge mistake and that I'm signing my own death warrant. And then you'll go on to say how you're going to cut my heart out and feed it to some dog somewhere. Blah blah blah. Oh, I left out the part where you're secret police. Does that cover it?"

"You are dead."

Hawk gave a wave of his hand. "I must admit this is a good cover for an illegal gambling place. Who would suspect an electronics store?"

"Are you going to be leaving soon, Jake, or are you planning on purchasing something while you're there?" Ilse asked.

The Brit indicated to the owner. "Reach inside his jacket pocket and take out his weapon. And before you say anything, Kamal, don't tell me you're not packing because I know that you are. I'm not an idiot."

With a trembling hand, the owner followed his direction. It slipped beneath the lapel and came out, holding a black Glock.

"Give it to me," said Hawk, holding out his hand.

The man passed it over and Hawk placed it into his waistband. He said to Kamal, "All right, mate, time to answer a few questions."

"I will tell you nothing," he spat.

"That's not exactly what I wanted to hear," Hawk said and shot him in the leg.

Kamal cried out in pain and crumpled to the floor.

Hawk stepped closer to him, the weapon still raised. "Let's try again, shall we? When is the auction?"

"What auction? I don't know anything about an auction."

Hawk shot him again. Same leg, a little bit higher.

As the secret policeman grasped at his leg to try and stem the pain, Hawk asked once more, "When is the auction?"

"Tonight. It is tonight," Kamal gasped, his eyes full of pain.

"Is it at the high rise?"

"Yes."

"Why is Medvedev there?"

Kamal looked confused. "Who?"

"Viktor Medvedev. You know who he is? He's the guy who sells girls all over the world, so rich bastards like your boss can get even richer."

"Never heard of him." Kamal's eyes told of his lie.

Hawk's finger tightened on the trigger. "Shall we start on the other leg this time?"

The secret policeman's hand flew up. "No! All right, I have heard of him."

"Then tell me, what is he doing here?"

"There are people after him. He expects them to come. The girl. It's all about the girl."

"What about the girl?" asked Hawk.

"He believes she is the key to him killing them. But he has deliberately made himself a target along with Hakim Anwar. He figures it would be too much of a target to resist."

Hawk caught movement out of the corner of his eye. He turned his head and glared at one of the patrons.

"You keep moving like that, Mister, and I'll put a fucking bullet in you." The man paled and remained still. "Good choice."

94

Hawk turned his attention back to Kamal. "Tell me about security."

The secret policeman swallowed nervously. Sweat formed on his brow from pain and, Hawk guessed, a good dose of fear. He swallowed before saying, "Medvedev has brought his own security. Some Russian, I forget what his name is."

"Ilya Noskov."

"That is him, he has a specialist team."

"How many?"

"Ten, maybe?"

"What about other security?" asked Hawk.

"Maybe ten more."

"Where do they keep the girls?"

Kamal shook his head. "I'm not sure, one of the floors."

"How many? How many girls?"

"I do not know. I only had to deal with the one."

Hawk stared at him for a moment before being convinced that he had all the information he was going to get out of the man. "Is there anything else that I need to know?"

Kamal shook his head to indicate the negative.

Ilse said over the comms, "Ask him about electronic security, Jake. See what he can give us."

"What about electronic security, Kamal? What does Ansari have?"

The pain in his leg was starting to really bite now and it showed. "The place is like a Fort. Once the alarm is raised, it shuts down. Elevators don't work, shutters come down over the doors to the outside. The emergency exits are locked, and an alarm goes out to Saudi special police. I guess you've heard of them."

Hawk had indeed heard of them. They were a special response force somewhat like SWAT and the Metropolitan Police's SCO19. "What is their response time?"

"Five minutes."

"Did you get that, Alpha Two?"

"I got it, Jake."

"Is Alpha One there, Alpha Two."

"Affirmative."

"I believe I have everything I'm going to get. Permission to continue."

Anja's voice came back, crisp and clear. "Permission granted."

"Copy, out."

Then without another word, Hawke shot Kamal in the head.

Widespread shock permeated the room within seconds, at witnessing the cold-blooded execution. The Brit looked around at all the men whose eyes were fixed on him. "I'm leaving now. But if I have any problems from any of you, you'll end up like our friend here on the floor. Not that I think I will, because if anyone finds out what's going on here, you will all end up in jail." He stared at the owner. "Is there going to be a problem?"

The scared man shook his head. "No, no problem."

"Good."

Hawk took his leave.

———

"I FEEL LIKE JAMES BOND," Hawk said as he looked at himself in the mirror. "Glasses, tie, cuff links, Handkerchief in my breast pocket. What do you think, Ilse?"

She smiled at him. "If I didn't know who you were, Jake, I'd rush you off to bed right now and rip that suit right off your body."

"Steady on, old girl. I'm not that kind of man."

She winked at him. "And I'm not that kind of woman, but I can make an exception. And like I said, if I didn't know it was you."

96

Hawk looked at himself again in the mirror. Even he had trouble recognizing himself. The MI6 Special Activities division had certainly outdone themselves this time around. The disguises for each of them were absolutely immaculate. So good, in fact, that even the most up-to-date facial recognition software would not recognize them. His smile broadened. "I do look good, don't I?"

"When you've finished ogling yourself in that mirror, Mr. Hawk, we still have things to discuss."

He turned and saw Anja walking into the room. Except it didn't appear to be her, with long dark hair, dark blue dress, cut high enough not to reveal her cleavage. She saw the look in his eyes and before he could speak, she said, "If you call me a Bond girl, Mr. Hawk, I'm going to shoot you before we even get out the door."

He reached up and touched his glasses. "Wouldn't dream of it, boss."

They all wore glasses. The ones that were going inside anyway. Anja, Ilse, and Hawk. The glasses doubled as a camera, running a feed back to the OPS room in the embassy. Normally Ilse would have remained behind, but Anja had promoted Patience to run the operation.

Ilse had also been given hair extensions and different colored eyes to go with her makeover. All in all, not one of them resembled their original persons.

Hawk looked at the form-fitting dresses. "I have a question? Where are you ladies going to keep your weapons?"

"We're not taking any," Anja replied. "Neither are you."

"This just keeps getting better," Hawk said, gob smacked. "How about we don't wear any underwear, too. We'll go completely naked."

"Who's wearing underwear?" Anja asked.

Ilse replied, "Can't wear it with these dresses. It would show."

"Good grief."

Anja chuckled. "Don't fret, Jake, it's all good."

Hawk looked relieved. "Just as bloody well. So, who am I escorting?"

Another smile split Anja's lips. "I would be the lucky lady. We are Mister and Missus Webster from Sussex."

"Why would a married couple from Sussex be in Saudi Arabia buying girls?"

"To add to our string of high-class prostitutes, darling."

"Sounds interesting. But not as interesting as our backup plan if we get rumbled."

"We'd better not get 'rumbled' then, best we? Are you ready?"

"Baby, I'm always ready."

"Don't push it."

CHAPTER NINE

Riyadh, Saudi Arabia

THE MAN SMILED AT THEM. "Welcome Mr. and Mrs. Webster. Please take the elevator on the left. Go all the way to the ballroom on the 80th floor."

Anja put away the fake invitation and returned the man's smile. "Thank you, kind sir."

As they walked to the elevator, Hawk said, "Patience, have you hacked into that security vision yet?"

"Almost done, Jake."

Behind him he could hear Ilse's high heels on the marble floor. As they approached the bank of elevators, he turned and said, "Posh place, isn't it?"

Hawk hit the elevator call button and they stood there waiting for it to arrive. The door dinged open, and they climbed into the glass walled car. The Brit opened his mouth to speak, but on the other end of the comm, Patience must have sensed something. "No one talk. I'm picking up radio signals from inside the elevator. I think there might be a listening device installed."

Out of habit, Hawk looked around the elevator, looking for a good place for the hidden mic.

Anja said, "How exciting I've never been up this high before. I've heard you can see the whole of Riyadh from up here."

"Speak for yourself. I get vertigo when I get above three floors," the Brit replied.

The Talon commander grabbed him by the arm and lay her head upon his shoulder. "Just relax, darling, you'll be fine."

He placed his hand on hers and looked across at Ilse. "What about you, young lady? Do you like heights?"

"I'm alright as long as I'm not near the edge."

"Yes, the edge is a killer."

The elevator slowed to a stop with a little jolt at the end. Then the doors spread wide. Before them lay a large room with polished floors and pillars with gilt running up and down them. Large panes of glass gave an almost 360-degree view of the city which was lit up like a Christmas tree. Ladies and gentlemen mingled, many seated at numerous tables, as well as standing with each other, talking, laughing.

"Can I see your invitation, please?" the voice had an accent. Definitely Russian.

Here goes, thought Hawk.

Anja and Ilse retrieved their invitations from their purses and showed the man. Hawk noted the telltale bulge of a holstered handgun tucked away in his jacket. He also had a comms setup. Glancing quickly down at the invitations, he then nodded his satisfaction. "Thank you. Please enjoy your evening."

As they walked off Hawk said in a low voice, "Patience, that fellow had an earpiece in. See if you can pick up the signal. Maybe listen to their chatter."

"On it, Jake. Oh, and you'll be interested to know I've been able to crack the security system and access the cameras. I can see everything that you do. Through your glasses and the cameras."

"I'll dance at your wedding, girl."

"And how about we kick things off with Dirk Gardner. American billionaire who runs a variety of adult entertainment parlors in Texas under the close care of the governor. Well, the last several governors, actually."

"That's a good start," Hawk muttered.

"But wait, let's look behind door number two. To your left is Vadim Portnov, Russian Oligarch. Again, another reveler in the adult entertainment business. However, his turnover in girls is horrific. Once every three months he cleans house. The bastard is a serial killer."

"Remind me to repay the debt before we leave."

"Over at the far wall I believe you know Hakim Anwar?"

"Yes, that bastard."

Patience continued, "I could go on the list is long. But I'm guessing there's only maybe two or three people you're interested in."

"Do you see Viktor Medvedev yet?" Anja asked.

"Not yet. I'll let you know when I do."

Suddenly Hawk's expression changed. "Will you get a look at this fucking scouser? I should go over there and punch his fucking lights out."

Anja glanced in the direction that Hawk was looking. A man wearing a black suit was sidled up to Ilse, his right hand tracing a line down the center of her buttocks over the silky fabric of her dress.

"Leave it, Jake. She can take care of herself."

And as if on cue her right hand shot out and grabbed the man hard in his crotch. The man stiffened as she leaned in close and whispered something in his ear. By the time she was finished, his face was red, and he slunk away when she let him go.

"I guess she can."

They moved through the crowd, taking a glass of champagne from a passing waiter. Hawk took a sip.

"Amazing what you can get away with when you're part of the family," he said referring to the alcohol which was totally banned in the country.

"I guess if you're going to break the law you might as well go all the way," Anja said. She took a sip. "I'm impressed, it's the good stuff."

"I do not believe we have met," a voice from behind the pair said.

They both turned and immediately Anja reached for Hawk's hand. She said, "Jack and Erika Webster."

Lars Akker smiled. "Pleased to meet you. Is that a German accent I hear?"

"It is."

He looked at Hawk. "Your husband is British, I assume?"

Anja squeezed Hawk's hand. The last thing she needed was for him to go hard at the man he most wanted to kill. "Yes, he is."

"Does he speak? Or is it his beautiful wife who does all the talking?"

Keep it up and I'll rip your fucking throat out. "I speak when I have something to say," said Hawk.

The two men locked stares for a long moment before Anja broke into their contest. "And where might you be from?"

Akker flicked his gaze in her direction. "I am from everywhere. My work takes me all over the world."

Not for much longer, Hawk thought.

"Jake, I think I've found where they are holding the girls," Patience's voice broke through his dark thoughts. "The floor below you. It looks like they keep them in separate rooms."

Hawk said, "Sorry, I need to go to the bathroom. You don't happen to know where it is, old chap?"

Akker nodded. "I most certainly do. It's over by the stairwell."

He glanced at Anja who gave a slight nod to tell him that she would be all right. Then, on cue, Ilse appeared. "Erika. We meet again."

Lars Akker smiled broadly. "What a lucky evening it is. Two lovely ladies to share a glass of champagne with."

"Or a jail cell," Hawk said, and strode off.

As he walked towards the door accessing the stairwell, he heard a man make an announcement. "Ladies and gentlemen, the auction shall commence shortly. Tonight, we have ten girls for your bidding pleasure. Have a great evening."

Hawk slipped through the door and onto the stairs, making his way down to the landing on the next floor. Trying the door handle, he found it turned easily. The whole floor on the other side of the door appeared to be empty. But he could hear voices further along, somewhere behind the wall. "What can you see, Patience?"

"You're OK for the moment. They're in a room around the corner."

Hawk made his way along the hallway until he reached the first door. He gently tried the handle. It was locked. Then he noticed it had an electronic key. "Can you get me into this room?"

"Give me a minute, I'll see what I can do."

"I'd like to think it'd take less than a minute."

Patience said, "If you keep talking to me, it'll take longer."

While he waited for Patience to unlock the door, he heard the voices of two men getting louder as they approached, with them a woman's voice, panicked, scared.

He spoke softly into his comms, "You had better get me in that door now."

"I'm going as fast as I can, Jake."

"Meanwhile, I'm standing here with my dick in my hand and no gun."

"I would have thought that was the only weapon you needed, Jake."

The voices were getting louder. "Come on, girl, get me in there."

As he surmised by the voices, two men and a woman appeared around the corner at the end of the hallway. Hawk pushed himself back into the foot-deep recess, which was barely enough to hide his form.

His impatience was beginning to build, knowing that once they reached him, he was done for. However, the trio stopped, but Hawk was unwilling to risk taking a peek. "What are they doing?" he whispered.

"They stopped at the elevators."

"Thank Christ for that."

The chime sounded and the doors slid open, the voices growing softer as the doors closed behind them. The elevator began its journey upwards one floor. Meanwhile behind Jake, the lock beeped, indicating that it was now open.

Backing into the room like he was meant to be there, he closed the door behind him. Turning to scan his surroundings, he took in a short passage which opened out into a larger room. Moving quickly forward, he observed a young woman sitting in the lounge chair. Something about her didn't look right. Her head was lolled to one side.

Hawk held a finger up to his lips as he approached her, but she just looked at him with a thousand-yard stare. He said into his comms, "It looks like they've been drugged."

"What about the other girl? The one that was out in the hallway."

"They probably screwed up and didn't give her enough. This young lady in here, she's pretty much high as a kite. I'll see if I can get anything out of her."

The Brit kneeled beside her, looking up into her eyes. He placed a hand under her chin, gently lifting her head so he could see better. There was a faint recognition there, and she said, "*Ciao, chi sei.*"

"She's Italian."

"Hold her head up a bit more. I'll see if I can get a picture," Patience said.

Hawk had forgotten that the glasses doubled as cameras. He held her head as still as he could, and then Patience came back to him. "Got it, Jake."

The Brit stared hard at the drugged woman. "Hey, do you understand English?"

Her eyes seemed like they were rolling in her head. "Si."

"What is your name?"

She gave him a broad grin. "*Il mio nome è gattina.*"

"What did she say?"

"She said her name is Kitten."

Hawk's shoulders slumped. "Bollocks. I'm not going to get anything out of her. Get me into another room."

"I'll work on the next one along. It should be open by the time you get there."

Hawk opened the door, but before stepping out, he asked, "Is the hallway clear?"

"Yes, and the next door along is open."

As he eased himself into the room, he was surprised by the girl that was in there. She took one look at him and started screaming at the top of her lungs. "What do you want? What do you want? Get out!"

Hawk held up his hand and said, "Take it easy. I'm here to help."

She stopped yelling at confused look on her face. "You are here to help me?"

"Yes," Hawk lied. "What's your name?"

"Elizabeth Turner."

She had an American accent. "Where are you from?"

"Kentucky."

"Why aren't you drugged like the others?"

"I pretended to take whatever it was in the pills they gave us. But I didn't do it."

Hawk nodded. He pointed at the green dress she wore. "Lift it up."

"Jake, we don't have time for this. They'll be back for the next girl soon."

Elizabeth looked at him funny. "Are you some kind of perv?"

"Do you have a tattoo. Did they tattoo you?"

She shook her head. "No."

"What about the other girls?"

"Not that I'm aware of."

"Do you *know* the other girls?"

Her head bobbed up and down once. "Yes."

"There is a British girl. Polly White."

"I don't know her name but there is a British girl here."

"Where?"

"In the room next to this one."

"Wait here," he said to her.

"You're not leaving me, are you?" Elizabeth asked terrified at the thought.

"No, I'll be right back." Another lie. "Patience, get the door on the room next to this one. The package is in there."

Less than a minute later he was in the room staring at another young woman who was drugged. "Well, this is fucked."

Hawk went back to the room that he had just left and found Elizabeth sitting on the side of the bed. "It wasn't her. Is she in one of the other rooms?"

She shook her head. "No, there was only one British girl. If she was here, then someone has taken her."

"Shit," Hawk hissed. Then he said into his comms, "The package is not here."

BOTH ANJA and Ilse heard the radio traffic and it made them pause. Maybe Hawk was wrong. Maybe she was in one of the other rooms. Anja said, "Check the other rooms, Jake. You have to make sure."

"Yes, ma'am."

"Hold it, Jake, the guards are coming back," Patience said urgently.

"Of course, they are," Anja muttered with a shake of her head.

The first auction was over. The "item" had been bought by a man from Latvia for $80,000.

Anja's eyes drifted back to Medvedev. Beside her, Ilse said, "Now is not the time. Remember, they are looking for us."

Her jaw set firm and she said, "Jake, find that bloody girl."

———

"THEY'RE COMING into the room, Jake," Patience said urgently.

Hawk glanced at Elizabeth. "They can't see me. Just relax and everything will be fine."

She looked doubtfully at the man she hoped was going to save her. "I—I can't go with them."

"You'll be fine," Hawk lied. He hated himself for it, but Polly White was the mission. The others would be passed on to the correct authorities and be picked up.

He slipped into the bathroom and closed the door almost all the way, leaving a crack he could see out of. The door to Elizabeth's room opened, and two men entered. Hawk heard one say, "She looks too alert."

"Did you take your medication?" the other asked.

"No."

"Where is it?"

"I threw them away."

Hawk watched as one of the men reached into his pocket. "It's a good thing I always carry a syringe."

The man moved to stick her with it. "Help me! Please help me."

Hawk knew what she was doing and muttered a curse. She was going to blow everything out of the water.

"Help me!"

"Will you listen to that, she says it like someone is listening," the man with the needle joked.

Elizabeth was desperate. "There is. He's in the bathroom."

The two men looked at each other and the one without the needle drew a handgun from beneath his coat. "Wait here."

As he approached the bathroom door, Hawk looked around for something to use as a weapon. Then he saw the long thin handle on one of the vanity drawers. The Brit hurried over to it and with one heave, it came free with a splintering of wood. Before the door opened, Hawk climbed into the shower and waited.

He felt the door swing open slowly, the displacement of the air inside the room noticeable. Bracing himself, the Brit waited for the man to appear. And when he did, he swung with all his might at the man's face.

The surprise was complete, the man's eyes widened just before the metal object impact across the bridge of his nose. Blood sprayed everywhere and the man went down hard. His handgun fell to the floor, and Hawk swiftly bent down and picked it up.

Not waiting, he stepped out into the main room. The weapon raised and pointed straight at the other man holding the syringe.

The man was left with two choices. Either put up his hands, or go for his gun and try to extricate himself from the mess he was in. One was smart, the other was not so smart, and from Hawk's experiences, when given those options, they always chose the stupid way.

The man dropped the syringe and went for his weapon, the coat flap being forced back as his hand dove for the weapon's grip.

"Don't!" Hawk snapped.

But the man wasn't listening. He could only focus on Hawk's weapon and wasn't about to let him get away with whatever he intended to do. Perhaps the fear of his bosses far outweighed the fear of dying.

Hawk cursed and squeezed the trigger, the shot rocking the room. The bullet punched into the man's chest, forcing him back before he could even touch his handgun. He fell onto the sofa and remained still.

Elizabeth cried out in fear at the violent exchange she had witnessed. Hawk looked at her and said, "Girl, I need you to calm down right now. Sit down over there on that chair and do not move."

"But—but you killed him."

"There was nothing I could do about that, but what happens next could mean life and death for either of us."

She nodded jerkily and sat down on the chair while Hawk said into his comms, "Heads up everybody. We're about to have an issue."

"Copy that." It was Ilse. "What do you suggest?"

"Shit is about to come down from a great height. I suggest you two ladies get out now while you can."

"What about you?"

"I have one more avenue to explore to see if I can locate Polly White. If it, too, is a dead end, I'll be out of here right behind you."

"Make sure you are," Anja said.

Hawk turned and strode back to the bathroom where he'd left the unconscious man. Stepping over the supine form, he bent and pulled him up by the collar, dragging him into the shower before turning the faucet on full. The cold water hit the man full in the face, pink water circling the drain, and coughing and spluttering, the man came back to consciousness.

Hawk shut the water off before leaning down and slapping him across the face. "Listen up, asshole. I'm going to ask you a question. You answer it and you might just live through it."

"I know nothing," the man spat in Russian.

"Wrong answer." The Brit hit him on his broken nose with the barrel of the gun in his hand.

Howling in agony, the man's body rose from the floor as pain coursed through his head. "Oww, what are you doing?"

"There was a British girl, Polly White. Where is she?"

The man gave him a hard stare. "I don't know what you're talking about."

"Why is it people always choose the hard way?" This time, Hawk placed the barrel of the handgun against the Russian's upper thigh. The weapon discharged and the man thrashed around violently. With a clenched fist Hawk hit him in the face, stunning him. "Try again asshole."

"She's not here, she's gone."

"Gone where?"

"I don't know."

"Who took her?"

"I don't know."

He knocked him out.

"I have an update," the Brit said, standing up and straightening his clothes. "The girl isn't here. She's been taken away." He placed his gun on the benchtop and closed the door, taking the opportunity to use the facilities while he was there.

Instead of Anja, or Isle replying, the voice he heard was from Patience. "Jake, we've got a problem."

CHAPTER TEN

Riyadh, Saudi Arabia

ANJA AND ILSE stared at the four, armed men standing before them. Each of them had their weapon drawn and pointed in their direction. The Talon commander recognized one of them right off. It was Ilya Noskov. They parted as Medvedev presented himself front and center. "Well, well, well. Hello, Miss Meyer."

She shook her head. "What gave it away?"

"It took a little bit, but we knew you were coming so we just had to look for the right people. Nice disguises, by the way."

Anja glanced left and right, trying to calculate her chances if she started something.

"I don't think it's such a wise move to try anything at this moment," Medvedev cautioned. "I've been quiet. Where is Jacob? I haven't seen him for a while."

"He's not far away."

The crowd was starting to back off and give them some room. Dasan Ansari stepped forward to join the others. "Are these the ones you were looking for, Viktor?"

Medvedev nodded. "These are the ones. Hawk is still here somewhere."

"Hawk is here?" Lars Akker called over to them.

"He is, Lars. Would you like us to keep him for you?"

"I don't mind, as long as he is dead."

"If we get him, consider his life a present."

Anja said, "You know, Viktor, you shouldn't make promises that you can't keep."

The killer smiled. "Who said I can't keep it?"

"As long as I've known Jake, which is not that long, I've found him a very resourceful man. Which means at any moment he could kill you where you stand."

Medvedev glanced at Noskov. "Find him."

"Is he the man who replaced Federov? Ilya Noskov?"

"I'm impressed you've done your homework."

"Well, I figured after Jake killed Federov, you'd have to replace him. Although I didn't expect it to be this quick."

Medvedev raised his eyebrows. "Leonid is dead?"

"Died of wounds," Anja lied.

"So sad, he was a good man. Now, what to do with you and your friend?"

When Anja moved, it was like lightning streaking across the sky. Her left foot came up, complete with high heel shoe attached to it. The fabric of her dress split down the side freeing her leg for the movement. Her foot crashed against the jaw of one of the armed men. The heel tore into his cheek, snagging against teeth. He cried out in pain, grasping at his face as he reeled away, the gun spilling from his hand. Blood ran through the man's fingers as he sank to his knees.

Anja ripped the bottom half of her skirt away. Revealing Lycra tights that stopped halfway up her calves.

Next, she dropped low, sweeping her right leg, taking the feet out from under a second shooter. The man cried out in alarm as he fell to the floor, and Anja twisted, then dropped the heel square onto his windpipe. Immediately, he began gagging for breath.

While the onlookers were stunned by what had just happened, Ilse herself had ripped the bottom half of her dress away, revealing similar tights to those that her boss wore. She stepped forward and kneed the third shooter in the groin. The man gagged as pain shot through his private area, hands dropping to clutch at his wounded pride at the same time as he sank to his knees.

Ilse brought up her knee. It crashed into the man's jaw, breaking it in two places. She bent and scooped up the weapon that had fallen from the man's grasp as the lights went out in his head.

As she came up, she was just in time to see another of Noskov's Russians withdrawing a weapon from beneath his jacket. She targeted center mass and squeezed the trigger twice. He crashed back, the gun dropping from lifeless fingers.

Anja picked up one for herself and brought it up to shoot Medvedev. However, she wasn't quick enough for one of Ansari's men had produced his own handgun and opened fire in her direction. She felt the heat of the bullet fan her face, and dove for the floor as the man fired three more rounds.

Those plowed into the crowd behind them, killing one of the bystanders. Chaos ensued as a wholesale panic set in and a human tide began washing towards the exits.

Anja spun onto her back, lifting the weapon in her right hand. She fired twice and saw the man reel around to his left as a bullet took him in the shoulder. She paused marginally, and then fired again, watching her round impact the back of the shooter's head. It punched clear through his skull blowing out of his forehead, popping eyeballs to leave dangling on the optic nerves, spraying a panicked patron with blood and brain.

Then the situation escalated. Another of Ansari's men

produced a Skorpion machine pistol and started spraying it in their direction, cutting down anyone within range of the deadly hailstorm's path.

Both women scrambled for cover, and terrified people began screaming and falling as the deadly rounds found soft flesh. Anja dived nimbly behind an upturned table just as a line of holes stitched across it. Wood splinters erupted out the underside with the passing of each lethal round. Anja leaned around the ruined table and fired three shots at the crazed gunman.

The man immediately staggered under the impact of a round in his chest. He fought to bring the Skorpion to bear, but two well-aimed shots from Ilse ended the battle.

"Fucking bitch," the voice behind Anja hissed, accent thick with rage. She spun on the floor and looked up to see a man she assumed was one of Noskov's, aiming a handgun at her.

Before she could fire, his head snapped back as a bullet smashed into it. He fell backward and Anja glanced around to see where the shot had originated. She spotted the figure standing in the doorway of the stairwell, and breathed a sigh of relief.

Hawk was back.

———

THE SOUND of gunfire seemed to sweep down the stairs, the closed door between barely dampening the decibels. As Hawk climbed towards it, he had a weapon in each hand, stopping to grab the second one to free his hand before he ran towards the stairwell door.

Reaching out for the door handle, a bullet punched through the thin wood. Splinters sprayed across the landing as the bullet passed close to his ear. "Fuck me."

Hawk flung the door open, retrieved the second weapon, and looked on at the chaos of people running everywhere. Men stood like sentinels watching the macabre scene unfolding before them. Then he caught sight of a man standing over Anja, a weapon pointed at her.

Without conscious thought, muscle memory taking over, he raised the weapon. His finger squeezed the trigger and the handgun bucked in his fist. He saw the bullet smash into the man's head and then the body crumple to the ground.

Anja glanced around and looked at him. Ignoring her, he stepped out into the room, ready to do battle. "This is a fucking stupid idea, Jake."

He knew the women were pinned down and the only way to get them out was to draw the attention and focus of the shooters in the room. Methodically, he went to work, firing the weapons as he walked forward.

Like a hero out of an 80's action movie—Stallone, Schwarzenegger, Norris—Hawk seemed to grow a foot taller and bulletproof.

"Jake, get under cover," Ilse snapped at him when she noticed him moving.

"You and the boss head for the stairwell," he shot back as a Russian fell under his fire. "I've got this."

"The girl, Jake," Anja reminded him.

"She's not here. Now get."

One of Ansari's henchmen came at Hawk from his right, a knife raised in the air. As it plunged downward, the former SAS operative blocked it with the handgun he held in his left fist and drove the muzzle of the one in his right deep into the would-be killer's middle.

Hawk fired twice and he heard the man on the receiving end grunt audibly. The Talon operative shoved him out of the way and said, "Haven't you ever heard, never bring a knife to a gunfight?"

As he started to scan the room, he caught sight of Lars Akker.

"Not so fast, cock swallower," Hawk growled and took aim at the trafficker.

Before he could fire, Hawk was suddenly slammed sideways by another of Ansari's hired thugs. As he hit the floor hard, the guns in the former SAS man's grasp spilled free.

Shit!

Hawk rolled as the man atop him began throwing wild punches at his head. The killer slid sideways, dislodged by the momentum of the roll.

The Talon operative struck at the man's snarling face with his elbow. He felt the connection jar up into his humerus, the pain of which was less than that of the broken jaw sustained by his assailant. Hawk rolled back to his left and scooped up one of the spilled handguns before placing it against the side of the incapacitated killer's head and pulling the trigger.

Hawk glanced at the door for the stairwell. He saw that Ilse and Anja had almost made it. Just a few meters to go.

A bullet snapped loudly as it passed close to the Talon operative's head. He turned sharply and saw one of Noskov's men. This one was bigger than the others and carried what looked to be an AK-12. "Now where did you get that from?" Hawk hissed in a low voice.

He threw himself sideways as the weapon came to life. Bullets sliced through the air and buried into the wall adjacent to Hawk's position.

The Talon operative scrambled to hands and knees before launching himself into a headlong dive towards an upturned table. His shoulder hit a prone form when he landed. A woman lay there in a pool of her own blood.

"Jake, we've made it," Ilse said over the comms.

"Get to the roof," he snapped and went to fire at the big shooter then realized he was out of ammunition.

"Bollocks!"

Looking around, he searched his immediate vicinity for another weapon. He sighted the Skorpion on the floor and was about to lunge for it when the table was hammered by more gunfire. As bullets punched through it, Hawk made himself as small as possible, hoping that bullets wouldn't find flesh.

The firing stopped as the big shooter stopped to reload. Hawk made his move and scrambled from cover, diving across the debris-strewn floor.

The Talon operative's hand clamped on the grip of the machine pistol, his finger slipping through the trigger guard as he rolled onto his back, hoping like hell it was primed to fire.

Hawk aimed at the big Russian's chest just as the man finished reloading and opened fire once more. Bullets cut through the air all around Hawk, howling as they ricocheted off the floor.

The former SAS shooter squeezed the Skorpion's trigger, and it rattled to life, sending comforting shockwaves up his arm.

Rounds hit the big Russian hard, stitching a line from his crotch up to his left shoulder. He cried out in pain as he collapsed to the floor in an untidy heap.

Hawk came to his feet and hurried across to the fallen man who was bleeding out on the floor. Reaching down, he collected the AK-12 from beside the man, and started to run towards the stairwell. Just before he hit the door, he said, "Coming your way, boss."

The door flew open, and Hawk started up the stairs. A voice in his ear said, "We're on the roof, Jake."

"Roger that."

Behind him the door crashed back once more, and he could hear excited voices. He stopped and leaned over the rail. The AK came to life as he fired downwards before continuing his ascent once again.

Bursting onto the rooftop, he felt the blast of a stiff

breeze in the darkness. The city all around was lit like an inverted sky with colored stars winking all around.

Ilse and Anja were climbing into their parachutes, doing up the harness. Hawk jogged over to them and said, "At least the parachutes were here."

"I don't know why I agreed to this," Ilse said. "Base jumping from a tall building to get away isn't my thing."

The third parachute was Hawk's. it was a double harness so that he was able to hook up to Polly White who wasn't there. "Did you get a line on her?" Anja asked as she checked her harness.

"Not a thing. She—"

Gunfire erupted across the rooftop cutting Hawk off. He dropped the third parachute and scooped up the AK. "Get going!"

"Jake—" Anja protested.

"Fucking now!" he shouted as he opened fire at a shooter approaching their position.

He opened fire in the direction of the new threat then ducked behind an air-conditioning tower which took the full force of the fusillade.

Hawk looked back just in time to see Anja and Ilse go over the edge of the building. He hoped that they wouldn't be scraped off the pavement 80 floors below.

Now all he had to do was extricate himself from the predicament he was in.

Suddenly the firing stopped. "Are you still alive, Mister Hawk?"

The accent was Eastern European. "You Medvedev or Noskov?" Hawk called back.

"Does it matter?"

"I'll say Noskov. If you were the man, you'd be gloating about now."

"Your powers of deduction are quite good, Mister Hawk."

The voice was different.

"That you Viktor?" Hawk asked as he checked the rounds in the magazine of the AK. "You want to step out where I can see you?"

"Not particularly. Why don't you lay down your weapon and come out? You can go nowhere."

"I would if I could get my parachute on, you fucking twat," Hawk muttered to himself. "Patience, have you got something for me?"

"Sorry, Jake. Not unless you like jumping off a building without a parachute."

"Did the others get down?"

"We're almost there, Jake," Anja said. "Can you get to your parachute?"

He looked at it in the moonlight. "It might be a bit tight."

"What are you going to do?"

"Wing it," he said before throwing the AK aside and standing up, hands in the air.

In his comms he heard Ilse ask, "Patience, what is happening?"

"Jake just surrendered."

Hawk stepped out so he was more visible and walked forward. He stopped in front of Medvedev and his entourage. "How's it hanging?"

Noskov stepped forward and hit him in the middle, doubling him over. Hawk coughed and spluttered and took a moment to gather himself. When he straightened, he looked at the former Russian military man and said calmly, "That's one."

"What?"

"You only get one shot for free," Hawk explained. "The next one you pay for."

Noskov hit him again with the same result. When he'd finally gathered himself, Hawk glanced at Medvedev who seemed to be enjoying the spectacle. Then moving swiftly, his right fist came up and crashed against Medvedev's jaw.

The world-renowned criminal reeled back, staggering. Hawk was quickly grabbed by the remainder of Noskov's men who pinned his arms and brutally forced him to his knees.

Medvedev straightened and loomed menacingly over the kneeling Talon operative. Hawk looked him in the eye through the gloom and said, "I warned him."

Another Russian approached the group. "The women got away. The crazy bitches parachuted from the building."

Anger boiled inside the trafficker. His plan had been foiled to an extent but at least he had their main agent.

"Get him on his feet," Medvedev hissed. "Take him inside. I will deal with him there."

———

WHEN ANJA AND ILSE LANDED, they bundled up their parachutes and jumped into a Mercedes Benz van. As they sat, the interior light came on and they looked at each other for a moment, not quite believing what they had just done. Both were breathless. After a few heartbeats, Anja asked, "What's happened to Jake?"

"They're taking him inside," Patience said.

"Does he still have his ear bud?"

"As far as I know he must do. I can still hear him talking."

"Jake, can you hear me?" Anja asked.

There was silence from the other end which she waited for as long as she dared before saying, "Jake, if you can hear me, click your tongue."

The noise was faint, but it was there.

"We'll do what we can to get you out. Just hang in there."

Another faint click of the tongue.

"Patience, what assets do we have?" Anja queried.

"Nothing on hand except for your two operators," she responded.

"Then they'll have to do. We're on our way back."

"Yes, ma'am."

Sudden static broke through their comms, followed by a deathly silence. Ilse looked at her boss, concern on her face. She said, "Patience, was that what I think it was?"

"Yes. We just lost communication with Jake."

HAWK KNEW they'd find the ear bud. It was only a matter of time. And he wasn't surprised once they got him into the light that they discovered it straight away. Noskov held it up in front of his face, dropped it on the floor, and then stomped on it with his heel. He gave Hawk his smug smile, and the former SAS operator had to restrain himself from trying to wipe it off.

When they arrived back at the grand room where the auction had been held, they found it was mostly clear, apart from the dead and the wounded. Medvedev looked around, and said to Ansari, "You need to get this cleared up."

The man glared at Hawk and said, "What about him?"

"What about him?" Medvedev said repeating the question.

"He must pay for what he has done. It is my right to have him."

The Russian trafficker took a few moments to consider this. He gave a slow nod and said, "Can you be trusted to deal with it properly?"

The Saudi man felt insulted but swallowed his ire, dipping his head. "I cannot guarantee it will be swift, but he will be dealt with. We have numerous deep dark holes that can keep this man safe and away from prying eyes while we deal with him."

"Fine then I will gift him to you." Medvedev turned and stared at Anwar. "But I want your business."

The man chuckled at the joke, turning when he realized that Medvedev wasn't laughing with him. His eyes widened. "You are serious? You expect to gain all of my business?"

"Yes. From now on, your business is mine, you will work for me. Consider it penance."

"But I have done nothing wrong. There should be no —what you call penance—due," he retorted.

"If it wasn't for you, we wouldn't be in the predicament we now find ourselves in," Medvedev snapped.

"You can't seriously be blaming this on me." The man's face and tone were incredulous.

"But I can and I do. The man who provided the mercenaries with the information about the British girl was in your employ. He knew about it when he was captured by them. You should have chosen better. Things like that put my whole network at risk."

"You'll get nothing of mine," Anwar said heatedly.

Medvedev sighed. "You will be paid well, but in return, you shall work for me."

"No," Anwar snapped.

"Ilya."

The Russian's hand blurred and reappeared with a gun. There was no hesitation just cold calculation as he shot Anwar in the head.

The two remaining men stood looking at the fallen man, taking in the blood pooling around his head. Hawk looked at Medvedev and said, "I guess this is what they call a hostile takeover."

"Shut up," Akker snapped, giving him a clip up the back of the head.

Medvedev suddenly looked bored. He glanced at his watch and said abruptly, "I must go. Good evening."

As he and his Russian bodyguards walked away, Hawk called after him, "Be seeing you, Viktor."

"Maybe in the afterlife," Medvedev called out without looking back.

"Yeah, in Hell."

CHAPTER ELEVEN

Djibouti, Two Weeks Later

"ANWAR IS DEAD," Ilse said to Anja, taking a few steps around the room. "The Saudis found his body the day after the operation. It's taken them all this time to identify him."

"Well I guess we can cross him off our list. It looks like Medvedev has put things together and isn't very forgiving."

"Is there anything on Jake?" Anja asked.

Ilse shook her head. "Nothing I'm afraid. I hated leaving him there."

Her commander nodded. They'd had to leave because things were getting too hot to stay. That was how they found themselves back in Djibouti. "We had no choice. All we can do is keep looking."

"Yes, but I still feel helpless."

"Let's hope Thurston's man on the ground can come up with something." She paused and then asked, "Where are we on Polly White?"

Ilse winced. This was another direction they were copping heat from. "Not very far, I'm afraid. We're trying to work out the movements of where she was sent, but we can't get anything. We're also still drawing heat from the British government through MI6."

"Just keep reminding them that it wasn't our fault. And we didn't pay."

"Yes, ma'am."

"Do you still have contacts from the old days?"

Ilse nodded. "Some."

"Reach out to them, find me something."

"Yes, ma'am."

Popping his head through the doorway, Karl said, "I think I might have something."

Anja nodded, beckoning him in to the room to give them an update. "I'm listening."

"I've been trawling through hours and hours of security footage from around the tower, where Ansari lives. Tracing the comings and goings of different vehicles and it was hopeless. So I changed my search parameters. Long story short, three days after everything had cooled down, a black Range Rover left the building and drove out into the desert."

"Where did it go?" asked Ilse.

Under his arm, Karl held a laptop. He placed it on the desk in front of them and opened it up. A few keystrokes later and a satellite picture appeared. "I'm not totally sure, but this might be the area in question."

"What is it?"

"I think it is Saudi Arabia's answer to a political prison. German intelligence has known about it for some time, so I reached out to a friend of mine who is still there. He confirmed my suspicions."

"How is Ansari involved in it?" Anja asked.

"His brother."

"Brother?"

"Stepbrother technically. His father had four wives. They gave him ten sons and five daughters. Ansari just happens to be the most infamous or what we would call the black sheep of the family."

"So we need to get in there and have a look," Ilse said, looking at her team mates for their concurrence.

"Someone does. I'm just not sure who." Karl's was nonplussed in his response.

Anja said, "I think I might know someone."

———

Riyadh, Saudi Arabia

"Fucking cock," Raymond 'Knocker' Jensen growled as he looked at the decrypted message. "Just a simple intel gathering operation they told me. And now they want me to break into a fucking prison and look around. Who the hell do they think I am? The Invisible Man or maybe even the Flash."

Patience grinned at him. "From what I've heard about your prowess, it should be a walk in the park."

"Or in this case a walk in prison. Bollocks."

He'd been in Saudi Arabia for the best part of a week and a half, trying to get a lead on what had happened to Hawk. Knocker had used previous contacts as well as numerous other people that he knew, but still he had nothing. He'd even reached out to Hawk's old contact and mate, Jocko Jackson. Nothing. Now there was this. And they wanted him to check it out.

Knocker sighed. "Tell them I'll go and investigate."

"How do you plan on getting in?" Patience asked.

He stared at her for a moment, before saying, "I have no frigging idea."

———

KNOCKER HAD three things going for him. His dark hair, his dark beard, and the Saudi Arabian armed forces colonel's uniform that he now wore. He knew that should he get caught he'd be screwed. Hell, he was screwed anyway, even if he wasn't wearing it. There was no comms of any kind, no contact to the outside world. It was a risk he couldn't afford. But there was a plan. Kind of.

The vehicle he was in slowed as it approached the large steel gate embedded in the 14-foot sandstone block wall. His driver was Jocko Jackson. "I don't know why I let you talk me into this, mucker," he growled.

"Because you miss the old days. I saw your record. I know what you're capable of."

"Ever since Jake turned up, it's been a shit couple of weeks. And now you're doing your best to try and get me killed."

"Cheer up. I'll buy you a beer when we're done."

"Just hope everything is in order. There's one thing out of place with that paperwork you've got, we're both fucked."

The vehicle stopped and they were approached by an armed guard. He spoke to them in Arabic and Knocker said, "I'm here to see the colonel," replying in the same tongue.

"Might I ask why?"

"You have a man here. A British man. I'm here to ask him a few questions."

"I don't know, sir."

"Let me see the colonel. He will know what I'm talking about."

"He—he is not here."

"Then who is in command?" Knocker demanded.

"Captain Hassan."

"Well, get him."

"But he is busy," the guard whined feeling the pressure of having to make a decision when he was used to only following orders.

Knocker played his trump card as he held up another piece of paper. "I have orders here from my superiors to speak with this man. Determine where he is from, and if need be, have him transported back to Riyadh for more intense questioning."

"But—"

"Let me in or you'll feel the wrath of General Abdullah."

The man paled. He turned and snarled at a second soldier who was watching on. Within moments, the doors were opening and they were able to drive through.

"Who the fuck is General Abdullah?" Jackson asked.

"No idea, but I figured either he'd know one or be too scared not to believe what I was saying."

Jackson brought the vehicle to a stop and, playing his part of faithful driver, came around to open the door to let Knocker out. The man from the guard post outside had followed them in and now stood to attention in front of the Team Reaper man.

"Sir, I will take you to see Captain Hassan."

Knocker shook his head. "Take me to see the prisoner. I have no time for being social."

"But, sir—"

Knocker looked at his watch. On the side of it was a small button. One press would activate a beacon transmitting to a helicopter standing by for a hasty exfil if required. The conditions for which included something going wrong, or him deeming it necessary to get Hawk out. That, of course, was part of his plan anyway.

The only downside, apart from getting killed if it went sideways, was that Jocko Jackson would never be able to work in Saudi Arabia again. Not that it mattered. For his help he was being well paid and had been offered a position at the Global Corporation.

"Sir? Is there something wrong?"

Knocker looked up. "I'm waiting for you to take me to the prisoner."

"What prisoner?"

"The British man I mentioned."

"Might you want to talk to another British man?" the guard asked.

Something was wrong. "What other British man?"

"We have one here who was brought in last year. Maybe it is him that you want?"

"No, the man was brought in recently."

"Sir, the guards were all told not to go anywhere near the other prisoner. He is only to be approached by the people from the General Intelligence Directorate."

Knocker was confused. What the hell was this? "Then why did you not tell me this before?"

"Because I was hoping you were mistaken. I cannot let you see the other man. Not if I want to keep out of the Directorate's bad books."

"Who ordered this?"

The guard opened his mouth to speak when a new voice stopped him. "What is going on here?"

Knocker and Jackson turned to see a thin man with a hawkish nose staring at them. "Who are you?" Knocker asked.

"I am Captain Hassan."

"Good, then you are the person I want to see."

The captain frowned. "What about?"

"You have a prisoner. A British man who was brought in recently. I wish to see him."

"I'm afraid that your request is denied. It is not possible to see him, Colonel," Hassan replied. "May I see some identification?"

Knocker gave him his forged ID and glanced at Jackson. Hassan looked it over before handing it back. "So what does military intelligence want with the prisoner?"

"Just to ask him a few questions. The general heard he was here and sent me to investigate the matter."

"You know the Directorate have given orders that no one is to see him?"

Knocker nodded. "I have been made aware of that fact recently."

"Then I'm afraid I cannot help you."

"Can't or won't?"

"Does it matter? The only person with the power to let you see him is my commanding officer and he will not be back until tomorrow."

"That will not do."

"I'm afraid it is all I can offer."

Knowing he wasn't getting anywhere, Knocker tried being forceful at the risk of overplaying his hand. "Then I'm afraid, Captain, that I will have to make it an order."

"But, sir—"

"Do it or I will shoot you in front of your men for disobeying a directive."

The man's shoulders slumped. "Follow me, sir."

A hint of relief touched the Brit as he and Jackson began to follow Hassan who took them inside a large wing of the prison. It was lined each side with cells; every now and then a moan could be heard emanating from one. At the end of the wing was a steel door which opened into a smaller cell corridor. On each side there were four doors.

"This is where we keep our special prisoners," Hassan said indicating with his hands to the steel barriers.

He stopped at the second on the left. Opened it with master key and stepped inside followed by the two Brits.

Knocker stopped and stared at the figure on the floor before him. He suddenly took out his handgun and rammed it into Hassan's stomach. "What fucking game are you playing?"

"I didn't authorize such a mission," Hank Jones growled savagely from the screen before Anja. "Do you have any idea what kind of shit storm this will cause if it all goes to hell, Miss Meyer?"

"It was made up on the fly, sir. We were acting on intelligence we received, and being an autonomous unit we kind of utilize what we can get at the time. And with all due respect, sir, we answer to Mary Thurston."

Ilse winced and waited for the bear of a man to come through the screen, but instead he nodded and said, "Tell me what you have so I can be prepared."

"I have two operatives inside the prison, presumably, looking for Jacob as we speak. Their job is to assess his condition and act accordingly. I'm quite sure Mister Jensen can manage."

Jones' eyes narrowed. "Did you say Jensen?"

"Yes, sir."

He groaned. "Son of a bitch. I'll have all British armed forces in the area put on standby."

"I don't think that will be necessary, sir. We have our own plan in effect and are prepared for all contingencies."

"You may think you are, Miss Meyer. But I think there is one contingency you left out."

"Which one, sir?"

"The one concerning Jensen."

———

Saudi Arabia

Knocker hit Hassan again making the captain stagger. Gone was the Arabic he'd been speaking, replaced by his unmistakable British accent. "This is not him, you cock.

Where the fuck is he before I ram this damned gun into your mouth and pull the trigger?"

"You—you are not—"

"I know what I am, now speak."

"He is in the cell next door to this one."

Knocker drew him close. "Right. You're going to let us into that one. If you even glance the wrong way, I'm going to put a bullet in you. Are you ready to die? Me and my friend here are."

"Steady on," Jackson said. "I'd rather die of old age."

"See?"

"Not what I said."

Knocker grabbed Hassan and shoved him towards the door, then put his handgun away. "Move your ass."

They exited the cell, locking it behind them. Hassan then moved to the next one along and with shaking hands proceeded to unlock it. They went inside and Knocker saw the figure hunched into a ball on the floor, clothes were dirty and torn as though whoever it was had been through a machine.

Knocker looked at Jackson. "Check him."

Jackson bent down beside the figure on the cold hard floor. "Jake?"

A moan.

"Jake, it's me."

The head moved and Jackson could see that it was indeed Hawk. An eye opened. "J—Jocko."

There were contusions and multiple abrasions on his face as well as dried blood. Jackson nodded. "Can you get up, mate, we're going to get you out of here."

Hawk tried to get to his feet, but was too weak to make the effort. With one glance, Knocker assessed the situation and drew his handgun. It rose and fell, Hassan grunting as his legs gave out. Knocker then stepped over beside Hawk and said, "Let's get him up."

Once they had Hawk on his feet, the Talon operative

painfully turned his head. His eyes took a while to focus before saying, "Knocker?"

"It's me, Jake."

"F—fuck, they sent the cavalry on this one."

"Who else do you think would be stupid enough to do something like this?"

"J—Jocko for starters," he managed before he started to sag.

"Let's get him out of here, Jocko, before all manner of shit comes down on us."

They almost made it, too.

Almost.

Djibouti

"I have just intercepted a warning signal from the prison to the nearby army barracks, ma'am," Karl called out. "It looks as though our boys have been rumbled."

"Knocker has just activated his beacon," Ilse said, confirming that something was indeed afoot.

"Where is it?" Anja asked.

"Still inside the prison but it looks as if they are mobile."

Anja said into the mic on her headset, "Striker One-One this is Alpha One, copy?"

"Copy, Alpha One."

"Are you getting the signal?"

"Yes, ma'am, we're spinning up as we speak."

"Roger that. Break. Eagle One, copy?"

"I'm here, ma'am," Grizz Harvey replied.

"How does it feel to be back downrange?"

"Better than the hospital, ma'am."

"We have no idea what you're flying into so keep your guard up."

"We've got this, ma'am."

"Good to hear, Eagle One. Alpha One out."

Anja turned back to her people. "Give me an update."

Ilse said, "It looks like they are out of the prison and headed into the desert. God knows what's following them."

"How far out is the helo?"

"It's lifting off, now," Karl replied. "Maybe ten minutes."

"Thank you. Let's hope they're not in too much trouble."

———

Saudi Arabia

"Never could shoot for shit," Hawk groaned as Knocker ducked down in the rear seat beside him.

Bullets hammered into the SUV as Jackson again swerved to the left. Knocker said, "You figure you can do better with a drunk at the wheel?"

"You want to drive," Jackson called over his shoulder as he swerved again.

"I would if I wasn't so busy," Knocker replied, firing his handgun at the armored vehicle following them. The slide snagged back, and he cursed. "Useless piece of shit."

"I could have told you that," Jackson called out.

Knocker looked out through the opening that had until recently held the rear window. There were three vehicles following them with heavily-armed men inside. He saw a shooter lean out of the lead vehicle and open fire.

The clatter of bullet strikes filled the inside of their SUV. It was only a matter of time before a bullet found a tire and put a stop to their dashing escape. Knocker looked at his watch. Hoping that the signal was still transmitting.

With a sudden jerk on the wheel, Jackson had the SUV in a violent turn towards the right. The vehicle leaned hard over and for a moment Knocker thought they would tip. A string of curses from Jackson filled the vehicle's interior.

"What the cocking hell?" Knocker growled.

"Sand cliff. Sorry."

It became obvious that the man driving the lead vehicle behind them wasn't as aware of his surroundings as Jackson was, for he simply vanished. "We're one less," Knocker shouted.

The SUV slowed abruptly. Jackson cursed once more and swung left trying to escape the loose patch of sand. The sound from the motor grew deep as it struggled to cope with the added pressure.

Behind them the remaining prison vehicles closed in. Knocker said in a loud voice, "Get us out of here, Jocko."

"What do you think I'm trying to do, you bloody scouser?"

Hawk gave a resigned chuckle from his slumped position. "Great, I'm going to die with you two wankers."

"Who said anything about dying?" Knocker growled, finally deciding to reload his weapon.

With a great surge, the SUV came free of the soft sand patch. The wheels bit on solid going and the motor roared happily. Bullets hammered into the rear panel and Knocker heard the unmistakable sound of escaping air. "We just lost a tire."

They were done, the SUV would just dig in. Up front, Jackson swung on the wheel as he floored the pedal. As Knocker stared out the front window, he realized what Jackson was about to do.

"Oh, cock!" he exclaimed just before the SUV went over the edge of the sand cliff.

Jackson fought with the vehicle all the way down the steep slope as he tried to stop it from rolling. It hit the bottom and the nose dug in before exploding through the sand. Jackson floored at once more, but the vehicle was going nowhere as its rear wheel bogged down.

He turned and looked over his shoulder. "I'm afraid that's it, we're done."

Up on top of the sand dune, the other two vehicles had come to a stop. The shooters inside all climbed out and stood on the edge, firing down at the SUV. Knocker muttered a curse and said, "Everybody out. This is the end of the line."

Jackson climbed out and took refuge behind the front of the car using the engine block as cover. Meanwhile, Knocker grabbed Hawk and dragged him free of the rear seat. He leaned him against the rear tire and said, "Stay put."

Hawk managed a grin but never moved.

Both Knocker and Jackson came up from behind the SUV and opened fire at the shooters above. Bullets kicked up sand around the Saudis, but the rounds were harmless.

Meanwhile the shooters up top had the advantage and the withering fire from their automatic weapons was having the desired effect. The two Brits took cover once more as incoming rounds grew fiercer.

Knocker dropped the magazine out of his handgun and replaced it with his last. "I'm out after this one."

Jackson nodded. "Me, too."

They stared at each other briefly before rising back up again and opening fire.

To their astonishment the Saudi shooters jerked wildly and started falling to the ground. Then came the roar as the Chinook helicopter flew low overhead, one of its miniguns still blazing fire.

Knocker watched as it circled back around and did another pass. This time, those still alive were sent fleeing across the desert on foot.

The Chinook circled back once more before setting

down, creating its own sandstorm. Four figures came out of the gloom. Grizz Harvey and his team. The big operator hurried over to Knocker. "How is he?"

"He could be worse. Let's get him aboard."

While the others held a rough perimeter, Harvey and Knocker helped Hawk to his feet. The Talon operative looked at Harvey and said, "Where the fuck have you been?"

The big man smiled and said to Knocker, "The bastard will be fine."

Somewhere in Europe

Viktor Medvedev stared at the report in his hand. He read it once more before looking up at Noskov. "This is true, yes?"

"As far as we can tell. He was broken out a few days ago."

The trafficker screwed up the piece of paper and threw it across the room. "I should have taken care of him myself."

"I can task a team to do that, sir. Fully autonomous with no contacts that might be traced back here. Maybe the Albanians."

"I want them all dealt with. They are making fools of us. They want to hunt me, then we will have them hunted. Do you have any idea where they are?"

"No, sir. But they will be found."

Medvedev nodded. "Fine. Do it one at a time. Break them down."

"Yes, sir."

"They will never stop Medusa."

CHAPTER TWELVE

Berlin, Germany

THE CANNULA SLID SMOOTHLY out of Hawk's arm as the nurse applied pressure to it to stop any bleeding its removal might cause. She smiled at him, showing white teeth and said, "Put your finger there, please."

While he held the small pad over the site, she took out a circular patch and peeled it. Then as he removed his finger, she placed it over the small hole. "There, now, you are to rest in bed for a few more days before you can go."

"Yes, ma'am," Hawk said and watched her leave the room.

"Nice ass," Ilse said.

Hawk smiled. "Yes—knock it off and fill me in some more. Polly White?"

"We have nothing on her yet. She's vanished."

"Lost into the underworld, you mean."

"Yes. I've been reaching out to some old contacts but so far they have produced no leads, so I have nothing."

"What about Ansari?"

"Disappeared after we got you out."

"I want that prick."

Ilse looked at the bruises still visible on Hawk's face. "We'll get him, Jake."

"And I'm guessing that there is no sign of Medvedev."

"No, he has gone to ground as usual."

"The girls?"

Ilse's face grew solemn.

"Is there any good fucking news?" he asked angrily running his right hand through his hair.

She reached out and took his other hand. "We'll get him, Jake. It's what we do."

He nodded. "Yeah, I'm just pissed about being laid up here. Don't think that I'm not grateful that I'm not still rotting in a Saudi prison, but sitting doing nothing makes me crazy."

Ilse let his hand go. "We could go to the cafeteria and get something to eat?"

"I'm stuck in bed, remember?"

"I won't tell if you don't. I'll find us some wheels."

Hawk climbed out of bed with only his underpants on. His top half rippled with his movement, muscles expanding and contracting. Ilse shook her head. "We'd better find you something to wear before the nurses start swooning."

"Very funny," he growled.

A few minutes later, Hawk had pants and a shirt on, ready for Ilse to wheel him out of his room and along the hallway to the elevator. The canteen was on the ground floor.

There was only a handful of people in the cafeteria, a fact which made Hawk happy. The last thing he wanted was to be amongst a crowd. "What do you want to eat?" Ilse asked.

"Why are you here?" he asked her as he stopped toying with the salt and pepper shakers on the table in front of him.

For a moment she was taken aback. "To make sure that you're all right."

"Is that all?"

"What do you mean?"

"You know what I mean, Ilse."

She sighed. "Damn it, Jake."

"It's not your fault, you know? It's a risk we all take."

"But we left you."

He nodded. "Yes, and it was the only thing you could have done."

A doctor entered the cafeteria and sat down two tables across from them to their right. Hawk stared at him.

"Are you listening, Jake?" Ilse asked.

His eyes flicked back to her. "Yes."

Another person entered, this one a nurse, female. She sat a couple of tables behind Ilse. "You know what," he said interrupting her. "I will have a coffee and a ham sandwich."

Ilse raised her eyebrows. "Oh. All right, but we finish this conversation when I return."

"I wouldn't have it any other way."

He watched her go up to the counter just as two more people entered. Doctors. One sat down behind him while the other went to a refrigerator to get a bottle of water before sitting a couple of tables to the left.

Hawk gripped the saltshaker. It might have been small, but it was heavy, solid. *All right, you've got me boxed, let's see what you do next.*

Each threat was Caucasian, not Middle Eastern which meant they weren't Saudis. The man with the water took a sip and the sleeve on his white coat slid back far enough to reveal a partial tattoo.

Hawk was trained to take things in, monitor his surroundings, be aware, which meant that even the fleeting glimpses told him more than he needed to know.

140

The guy was Albanian. The tattoo screamed it. Which meant they were mercenaries. But why were Albanian mercenaries here for him?

He glanced at Ilse who was oblivious to the situation. The last thing he wanted was for her to be caught in the center.

Hawk reached out and grabbed the saltshaker, tapping the top of it as though he was interested in it. Then he looked at the woman to his front and winked.

The Albanian woman lurched in her seat as she reached for the throwing knife at the nape of her neck, hidden beneath her long hair.

Hawk's shaker-filled hand whipped back then forward, his muscles acting like a spring-loaded catapult. As the object left his hand it tumbled through the air several times. The Albanian woman's knife had just come free of its sheath when the shaker hit her between the eyes.

She went down in a heap on the floor, the chair she'd been sitting on turning over, the knife spilling from her hand. But Hawk didn't see this, he was already moving for the second person on his left.

As he went he took the only improvised weapon he could find. The pepper shaker.

The man reached for a silenced handgun, surprised at the sudden violence and explosive movements his target had just displayed. Hawk crashed across the table in front of the killer, his left hand clamping down on the Albanian's wrist behind his gun hand.

The Talon operative swung the pepper shaker overhand and brought it savagely down upon the killer's head.

Eyes rolled back and the man slumped to the floor. Hawk crashed down beside him, the table falling onto its side.

Hawk rolled and grabbed the suppressed handgun

which lay abandoned on the floor beside them. He grabbed it and turned and shot the man in the head.

Hawk covered his head as a tattoo of bullets hammered through the thin tabletop beside him. Then he rolled away from it and came up on a knee, bringing the handgun level. He saw the shooter, used the identification badge as a target, and placed three bullets around it.

"Jake, look out!" Ilse cried out.

He pivoted to see the final killer aiming at him with another suppressed handgun. There wasn't anything he could do; he'd either die or get lucky in this one moment. There was no in between.

Time slowed as Hawk saw the Albanian fire and the bullet leave the barrel. He braced himself for the impact but nothing happened.

It had missed.

Hawk didn't.

The handgun was fired three times, each bullet, punching into the would-be shooter's chest. The Albanian cried out in pain, then fell to the floor. Working on instinct, Hawk swept the rest of the room before relaxing his guard. The few customers who had not managed to escape already were now heading towards the cafeteria door in a swift procession.

He looked at Ilse. "Are you OK?"

For a moment she looked stunned, but soon gathered herself. "I'm alright. But what the hell was that?"

"I'm not sure. I think they're Albanian mercenaries."

He bent down and started to check the one closest to him. As he did so, he said to Ilse, "Check the woman. I'm not sure if I killed her with a saltshaker."

Ilse checked her for a pulse. "She's still alive."

Hawk lifted the sleeve of the man he'd been checking and found a tattoo which confirmed his suspicions. "Just as I thought. They're Albanian."

"No guessing as to why they were here," Ilse said shaking her head.

"Yes, they were placed just right. What now?"

"We get you out of here before the police arrive. It can be explained later."

"The woman."

"Get her in the wheelchair. We'll take her with us. Damn it, Jake, why can't you just be normal?"

———

"WHERE IS SHE?" Anja asked, picking up her cell and a closing a file folder she'd been perusing when they'd entered the room.

"In the interrogation room," Ilse replied. "She woke up on the way here. Luckily she was in the trunk of the car."

"And you say they're Albanian?"

"Yes."

The Talon commander looked at Hawk. "Damn it, Jake, why can't you be normal?"

"I'm thinking I've heard that somewhere before." He scratched his head as though trying to recall.

Anja sighed. "Get some rest. Ilse and I will question her."

"What about the authorities?"

"I'll deal with them. Now, rest."

Hawk left the room and went to lay down. The MI6 safehouse on Heiligendammer Straße wasn't short on them. The place was big enough for the team and the three permanent officers they had there. Not to mention the ones at the embassy.

Anja looked down and unlocked the screen on her cell before dialing. "Hello?"

"Gunther?"

"Yes."

"Anja Meyer. I need to speak to you."

"Now?"

"No. I'm in Berlin. Can we meet for coffee tomorrow or this evening?"

"How about dinner at eight?"

"Sounds lovely. I'll see you then."

"Anja?"

"Yes?"

"It's good to hear from you."

The call disconnected.

Gunther Altmann was the head of German Intelligence. If anyone could help her, it would be him. She looked at Ilse. "Let's go and question our prisoner."

———

THE PAIR TOOK the two vacant chairs on the opposite side of the table to their prisoner. Standing in the corner was Grizz Harvey for added security as well as his intimidation factor. But by just staring at the woman opposite her, Anja didn't think that she would be the sort who was easily intimidated.

The woman's dark hair was shoulder length, and her fine features belied her capabilities. The cold blue eyes, however, seemed almost bottomless.

"My name is Anja Meyer, but I guess you already know that."

The woman stared straight ahead at a point over Anja's shoulder.

"Not talking? I can understand that. The rest of your people have been killed in a failed attempt to take out one of my team. Screams amateur to me."

"What would you know, fucking bitch?" the woman snarled in Albanian.

"I know that you couldn't kill one man when you had him surrounded and outnumbered," Anja shot back at her

144

in her own language. The woman's expression changed and she fixed Anja with an icy look, but Anja ignored it, continuing, "Yes, I speak Albanian. And a shit load of other languages as well."

Beside Anja, Ilse switched to Albanian as well. "Would you like to tell us who hired you?"

"No."

"You know we'll find out eventually."

No answer.

"Was it Medvedev?"

Nothing.

"What about Noskov?"

Her eyes flickered.

Ilse nodded. "Noskov it is. Understandable. A man like him would have connections. What were your orders?"

Again, silence.

"How many of you are there?" Anja asked.

No answer.

Ilse looked at Anja. "Tough nut."

"Pretending to be. But I can see by the look in her eyes she's wavering."

Suddenly the woman's jaw set firm and her face grew contorted. Foam began emerging from between her lips and her body was soon shaking uncontrollably. "Grizz, quick."

The big operator lurched forward but it was too late. The cyanide had already taken effect. He looked at the dead woman and said, "That fucked that."

———

"THAT'S the last time I bring one back alive for you lot to interrogate," Hawk growled.

"Shut up, Jake," Anja growled, still angry about what had happened.

"What now?"

"I have a meeting tonight with the head of German Intelligence. I'll see what I can get out of him and try to smooth over the incident at the hospital."

"So where are we overall?" the former SAS man asked.

"We don't know how many of the Albanians there were, we have no idea where Polly White is, and as far as Medvedev is concerned, we've hit a brick fucking wall."

She was frustrated and rightfully so. Hawk thought for a moment then looked at Ilse and Karl. "Can I help with some of the intel?"

Karl said, "We've been trying to identify the possible buyers from the night of the auction. We've come up with a few names but as with everything else associated with Medusa, some names are hard to come by."

"Who do we have?"

Karl pointed at the large screen with the remote he held in his hand. "Dirk Gardner, American billionaire."

"Yeah, know him."

"Vadim Portnov, Anwar is dead, and Lars Akker."

"What about all the rest who were there?"

"We believe most of the rest are window dressing. All except these four."

The pictures flashed up. Hawk stared at them. "Have you sent them over for Federov to look at?"

Anja shook her head. "I was hoping we could do it without involving him. The man is a lech."

"Put me on a plane and I'll go talk to him," Hawk said. "It's only an hour there and back."

"There is a thing called Zoom."

"No, I'd rather do it in person."

Anja nodded and took out her cell. "All right."

He looked at Ilse. "Add Gardner and Portnov to the list of targets. I'd like to pay them a visit."

"Already done."

Anja hung up. "The jet will be ready in an hour. I'll notify the MI6 site you're on your way."

"Thank you, ma'am."

"Get me something, Jake. Even if you have to beat it out of that little weasel."

CHAPTER THIRTEEN

MI6 Secure Facility, Europe

WHEN THEY LET Hawk into the room, Federov was already waiting for him, seated at the stainless-steel table, chained to the bar running across it. He looked disappointed when he saw that it was Hawk entering.

"When they told me I had a visitor, I did not expect it would be you," he moaned.

The Talon operative tossed the folder on the table in front of himself as he sat down and said, "They sent me because I won't put up with your shit."

"I don't like you," Federov replied childishly. "Leave. I will talk only to Anja."

Hawk shook his head. "Not an option. I'm here, you talk to me."

"And what if I don't want to?"

The former SAS man leaned over the table. "Another thing that's not an option, Federov. We have a deal. If you don't live up to your deal, I'm going to find a deep dark hole and bury you neck deep in the fucking thing."

"All right, all right. What is it you want to know?"

Hawk opened the folder before him, then took out

seven pictures. "I want to know the names of these four men. I'm guessing you know each and every one of them."

Federov took his time, but in the end, he gave a slow nod. "I know them."

"Tell me their names and everything you know about them."

Federov tilted his head to one side. "Did you find the girl?"

"What girl would that be?"

"Polly White."

"No, they moved her."

"That is sad."

Hawk's ire rose.

"Just tell me who the people in the fucking pictures are." He stabbed a finger at the first photo in line. "Start with this guy."

"Vadim Portnov. Russian oligarch. Not the nicest of people. Bought a lot of girls from us because of his high turnover."

Hawk had put the first three pictures in the mix to make sure Federov wasn't lying. "Would he have taken Polly White?"

"Is that what this is? Are you trying to find out who might have taken the girl?"

"Yes," Hawk snapped. "Could it have been him?"

"How old was she again?" Federov asked nonchalantly.

"Early twenties."

Fedorov shook his head. "No. Portnov likes them younger. Eighteen or nineteen. He will not have her."

Hawk stabbed a finger at the next picture in line. "Him?"

Anwar.

"No. What is this? Are you trying to catch me out in a lie?"

"That's exactly what I'm trying to do, and if you do lie to me, like I said before, I'll bury you."

Hawk moved on to the next picture. "Tell me about him."

"Dirk Gardner. An American billionaire who uses his legitimate business to hide his dirty money. Involved in porn, strip joints, and underground prostitution. He will not have her either."

"You sound so sure?"

"He has a certain type. Polly White does not fit that type."

"What is his type?" Hawk gave the man a hard stare, communicating his displeasure with him should he lie.

"Black girls. African. Sudanese, Sierra Leone."

"Next one."

"How about I save you time and trouble with this silly game?" Federov said. He started going through the rest. "Jakov Krajl, Serbian. Arms trader and people trafficker. Likes German and Belgian girls because they are more sexually free. Or so he says. Rule him out. Daniel Linna, from Finland. His thing is Russian girls and some Italian. He stocks his brothels with them after he gets them hooked on drugs. Once they've passed their used by date, he dumps them on the streets. They're so hooked on shit that they ply their trade from the gutter just to get their next fix. That is before winter. By the time winter is done, most of them are dead from the cold."

Hawk felt his blood boil as Federov's callous narrative proved his knowledge of what was happening and at his lack of empathy.

The Russian continued. "Grigor Petrovski. Macedonian. I'm surprised he was even there. His main business is preying on refugees or Romanian girls. Although every now and then he will appear just to kiss Viktor's ass."

The Talon operative nodded. "That leaves this one."

Federov stared at the picture, his face stoic. For some

reason Hawk got the feeling that the Russian didn't like this man at all. "Who is he, Leonid?"

"Damyan Dragov. Bulgarian. If any one of these men has her, it will be him."

"Why do you say that?"

"The man is an animal—"

Hawk stared at him. "Are you saying you're not?"

"Compared to him, I am a saint."

"Let me be the judge of that. Continue."

"The man has his own Eastern European underground pornography network. Also brothels in Bulgaria. But he will want her for the other. How long has she been gone?"

"Almost three weeks."

"Then you don't have much time. She may already be dead."

"What do you mean?" Hawk asked.

"Dragov is a nasty man. You would do best to kill him given the chance. He has a taste for the—for giving his customers what they want."

"What is it that they want?"

"The exotic, Mister Hawk."

Hawk was getting angry again. "Just spell it out for me, Leonid. What does he specialize in?"

"Death. The man specializes in death. At the end of every scene, the girls are killed."

"The guy makes Snuff films?"

Federov nodded. "I'm afraid so."

Hawk sat for a moment, his mind whirring. Of course there was every possibility that Polly White wasn't with this guy. But could he afford to take that chance? Even if she wasn't, there was a possibility of saving others. Wasn't this what they did? "Tell me all you know, Leonid. Don't leave anything out."

———

The restaurant's mood lighting was provided by numerous scalloped sconces around the walls, with tasteful artworks centered in the spaces between them. Which to Anja seemed a waste because the lighting wasn't bright enough on the canvases to let anyone fully appreciate them. The maître d' station had a small lamp which gave off only a small circle of light, enough to be able to see the booking register.

Anja sipped her white wine while across from her, a solidly built, gray-haired man sloshed his red around in his mouth before swallowing. He placed the glass down on the pale red tablecloth and said, "It is good to see you, Anja. I trust everything is well with you?"

"Yes, Gunther. I'm still fighting to right all the wrongs in the world."

"I was sorry to see you leave the service, but..." he let it hang not wanting to tear open old wounds.

"I've moved on from it. The job I have now suits me very well," she said with a dismissive wave of her hand.

"Which is?" The man seemed genuinely interested.

"I am in command of a team tasked with putting a dent in human trafficking. Namely, Medusa."

The man's face remained passive, but Anja could tell he knew more than he was letting on.

"A few weeks ago, I had a team—one man actually—run a mission into the Nubian Desert. That mission was the liberation of a number of girls who had been sold to Mustafa Osman. The outcome was successful, however there was one we were unable to locate. Her name is Polly White, the daughter of a British MP. Our intel had her trafficked to Saudi Arabia where we launched another operation."

"That was your people?" Gunther asked incredulously.

Anja nodded. "Not one of our better ones, I'm afraid."

The head of German intelligence shook his head. "No. It took a lot of courage to launch an operation on Saudi soil. I applaud you for that. Did you get her?"

"No. And we left one of our own behind at the time. Thankfully we were able to extricate him alive a few days ago. He was being held in a political prison outside of Riyadh."

"I heard whispers about that, too. It would seem that your team cares little about borders."

Anja gave him a wry smile. "What is it they say about permission and forgiveness?"

"Yes, I see." The German stroked his chin thoughtfully.

"We are working on dismantling Viktor Medvedev's empire from the ground up."

"Wait? Victor Medvedev is the head of Medusa?"

"Yes. I thought MI6 would have notified the intelligence services."

"We have heard nothing to confirm this."

"Then I do not know." She paused. "Now, about an incident in the hospital—"

Gunther held up his left hand to stop her. "I have a feeling what you're already going to tell me. This was your man?"

Anja nodded. "Yes. Him and a handful of Albanian mercenaries."

"I was looking at the camera feed. Your people took a prisoner."

"Before you ask, she's dead. Cyanide. I just wanted to let you know what happened so hopefully you can stop anything before it starts?"

"You are asking me to intervene, so your presence doesn't come out in public. Is that right?"

Anja nodded. "Yes, I am."

153

"The right thing to do would have been to notify us of your presence before this happened."

"How was I to know that this was going to happen, Gunther? Tell me that."

The man sipped his wine before sighing. "Is there anything else you wish?"

"If you could ask your agents to keep an ear open, they might find out something without knowing."

Gunther nodded slowly. "I can do that. Now, how about that dinner?"

Anja's cell buzzed. She looked at the screen and then back at Gunther and said, "I'm sorry I have to take this."

He held his hands apart in a helpless gesture. "Be my guest."

The Talon commander hit the answer button and said, "What is it, Jake?"

"I think I have a lead on where Polly White is."

Hope surged through Anja. "Where?"

"In Bulgaria with a man called Damyan Dragov. We don't have much time. We need to get her out of there now."

"All right, Jake. How far away are you?"

"About an hour."

"I'll see you then."

She disconnected the call and stared at Gunther. "Have you ever heard of a man called Damyan Dragov?"

The German intelligence boss frowned for several moments as he thought. "I think so. He is Bulgarian, if I'm right."

"Yes, that's right," Anja agreed. "Jake thinks he could have our missing girl."

Gunther's vice crew troubled. "Oh dear. If it is the man I think it is, then your girl is in very deep trouble indeed."

"That's what Jake said."

"Do you need some help locating him?" Gunther asked.

"If it is going to make our job easier, then yes, that would be appreciated. Thank you."

He gave her a grim smile. "First dinner, then work."

———

"I'M SORRY, Gunther, I'm afraid I've been careless," Anja apologized.

The fork stopped halfway to the German intelligence commander's mouth as he stared at Anja. He noted that her hands were now below the top of the table. "Anja, what is happening?"

"There is a table two to our left. Do you see it?"

Without looking, Gunther said, "Yes, it has a man and a woman sitting at."

"They are Albanian. I think they are part of the mercenary crew that came after Jake."

"That is inconvenient. We can't have a shootout in here. There are too many people."

"I believe they are after me. If I leave, they will follow. That will make everybody else safe."

Gunther shook his head. "No, we will finish our dinner, have another glass of wine and then we will leave."

"Gunther—"

The man held up a hand to silence her before reaching into his coat pocket to pull out his cell. He hit speed dial, waited for an answer and then said only a few words quietly. After he put the cell away again, he bowed his head graciously to Anja. "Everything will be taken care of. Now let's enjoy our food."

Without paying further attention to their observers, they took pleasure in each other's company and the delicious fare before them. After finishing their wine, they then placed their napkins on the table, waiting for the check before rising to leave. Once they had gathered their coats, Gunther helped Anja into hers before they stepped out into the cool Berlin night air. As they walked down the concrete steps to the sidewalk, Anja sensed they were being followed. Reaching into her handbag, she felt the reassuring grip of a SIG Sauer P365.

Gunther touched her arm. "Keep walking, my dear, all is under control."

Anja glanced around, and almost immediately picked out at least two undercover operatives. She glanced to her left and found another one, then ahead of them across the street was a fourth.

When they hit the sidewalk, they turned right, and their pace quickened. Behind them, she heard the couple's footsteps increase to keep pace with their own. She fought hard against the urge to stop, pull the handgun, and turn and fire. "Just a little more," Gunther said from beside her.

Then suddenly the trap was sprung. Armed agents and specialist forces seem to come from everywhere. The two Albanians were taken completely by surprise and had no hope of getting their weapons out. Instead, they stopped, feigned innocence with shock etched on their faces. Within moments, they had them face down on the hard cold concrete of the sidewalk. Their hands flexi cuffed behind their backs.

Gunther looked at Anja. "Do you wish to question them?"

"I don't think I have time. Will you let me know what you find out?"

"Indeed, I will."

"Thank you, Gunther."

———

ANJA, Ilse, Karl, Hawk, and Grizz Harvey gathered around to discuss the intel that Hawk had drawn from

Federov. Once on the plane, Hawk had called Ilse and informed her that they needed a package made up on Dragov. The folders were waiting for them at the briefing.

Looking down at the face staring back at him from a photo, the Talon operator asked, "Is this him?"

"Yes," replied Ilse.

"What do we know?"

"Dragov is wanted by Interpol and half a dozen other law enforcement agencies across Europe. He is the porn king of Bulgaria and specializes in what are known as snuff films. I think we all know what they are. Anyway, Leonid told Jake that if our lost girl is anywhere, it will be with him."

Hawk said, "We need to do all we can to find this scouser as soon as possible. If she isn't already dead, she won't be long for this world."

"Burgas in Bulgaria," Karl said. "It's on the Black Sea."

"Can we pin him down to a specific location?" Hawk asked, looking from one team member to the next in turn.

The former German intel man shook his head. "No. He has three residences there and spends time in all of them. There is no way of pinning him down until you get there."

Hawk nodded. "That's fine. As long as he's there, I'll find the bastard."

"You need to be aware he has local law enforcement on his payroll."

"They always do."

Anja said, "This needs to be surgical, Jake. Which is why you'll be on your own. Work a plan and I'll make it happen."

"Is that wise?" Harvey asked. "Especially after what he's already been through? Let a couple of us go as backup."

Anja shook her head. "No. I have another job for you,

Mister Harvey. It may be a little tricky, but we'll be running a parallel op."

"Do tell."

"Tonight while I was dining with an old friend from German Intelligence, our Albanian friends decided to partake of some gastronomic excellence, at the same restaurant. I want them found and taken out before they get lucky and kill one of us."

Hawk cut in with, "Huh? What does that mean in English?"

It was Ilse who spoke. "Hawk, she means dine on the fine food also." Directing her attention back to Anja she said, "Miss Meyer, we are already stretched thin. With the Bulgarian op, trying to find Ansari, and now this, it could possibly be a tipping point."

"I understand your concern. Forget Ansari for the moment. But the other two operations stay. You will run backup for Jake, and Karl will do what he can for Mister Harvey and his team. Getting rid of Dragov will save a lot of lives. And taking out the Albanians will save us."

"ROEs, ma'am?" Harvey asked.

"Terminate with extreme prejudice, Mister Harvey. Send Medvedev a message."

———

Somewhere in Europe

"I want a progress report, Ilya. Shouldn't we have heard something by now?"

"It would seem that either Anja Meyer and her team are far more resourceful than they have been given credit for or the Albanians are not what they claim to be."

"Which is it?"

"The former I'm afraid."

Medvedev sighed heavily. "Why won't these people just die?"

"Might I make a suggestion, sir?"

"What?" Medvedev's tone was curt.

"I think it is time for you to disappear for a while. Go completely dark. You hired me to run things, let me do it. The more you stay exposed, the more chance there is of them finding you."

"For how long?" Medvedev asked.

"For as long as possible. A year, maybe two."

The man's face grew red. "What? Impossible."

"The more you are exposed, sir, the bigger threat there is to the operation."

"It is my operation, Ilya, not yours. I will not hide like some frightened little schoolboy."

"Yes, sir."

Noskov stood there in front of his boss, waiting. Medvedev glared at him and snarled, "Was there something else?"

"Yes, sir."

"What?"

Noskov took out his weapon and shot Medvedev in the head.

———

Berlin, Germany

When Ilse entered the room Anja couldn't help but see the angst on her face. Or was it excitement? "What is it?"

"Viktor Medvedev's body was just dumped outside the National Museum in Warsaw."

A whole wave of emotions flooded through Anja at the news. She didn't know whether to feel happy, relieved, or disappointed at being robbed of the chance to do it herself. "What do we know?"

"Not a lot. When I heard the news I made a call before coming here. He was found there early this morning with a bullet hole in his head."

Could this be the end of Medusa? Anja stared at Ilse. "Hostile takeover?"

"Too early to tell. What do you want me to do?"

"Nothing. I'll monitor the situation. Is Jake in Bulgaria yet?"

"Almost there."

"Good. Does Karl have anything on the Albanians?"

"That is something else."

"What do you mean?" Anja asked noting the confused expression on Ilse's face.

"Karl is verifying some intel that came in last night. We should know more shortly."

"Intel from where?"

"We don't know. We're trying to work out if it is a trap or not. So far we have activity in the area but we're unsure who it is."

"Update me when you know."

"Do I tell the others about Medvedev?"

"Not yet. I need their full concentration on what they are doing."

"Yes, ma'am."

CHAPTER FOURTEEN

Burgas, Bulgaria

HAWK'S TARGET was Rumen Marinov. He lived in a small house on the outskirts of Burgas overlooking the Black Sea. It was a stone-built home with terracotta tiles on the rooftop. Out front was a long stone wall sited at the edge of the narrow laneway.

Marinov was Dragov's accountant, hence the luxurious seaside accommodations. Important to Dragov's businesses, some considered him a linchpin, and the four guards on the property reflected that status.

To the west the sun was sinking beyond the horizon. Hawk knew it would be a long night due to everything he had to do. He needed to get a location fix on Dragov to ascertain whether he was in possession of Polly White. If that went to plan, he then had to find and free her, if she was still alive, and then get back out of Burgas.

"Alpha Two, can you confirm just the four guards, over?"

"Confirm, Bravo One. ISR is showing four."

"What about inside the house?"

"Two signatures. Upstairs on the second floor. Same room."

"Copy that. I'm going in."

"Good luck, Jake."

"Just make sure the boat is there."

"Our contact has promised that it will be. Out."

Hawk got out of the SUV and hurried across the street where a steel gate gave pedestrian access through the stone wall. He could smell the salt water on the breeze as it gently brushed by.

He stopped at the gate and rattled it, trying to draw the attention of the nearby guard. The man stared at him before walking over. "Kakvo iskash?" What do you want?

"I'm looking for Mister Marinov."

"English? Go away."

Hawk brought the suppressed SIG free from where it was nestled and sent a bullet at the guard's head, snapping it back and he fell to the ground.

The Talon operator climbed over the fence and took the dead man's radio. He then walked swiftly towards the front of the house.

The next guard observed him on approach and walked to the to the top of the stairs leading to the stoop. "Koĭ si ti?"

The words had no sooner left his mouth when he died with a single slug to the brain.

Hawk stepped over the body and tried the doorknob. The heavy wood door swung open, and Hawk leaned down to drag the guard inside.

Pulling the door closed behind him, he said in a low voice, "I'm in. Where is he?"

"Second floor, third room on the right."

"Roger that."

The stairs to the upper level were to the left of the foyer and he began ascending them two at a time until he reached the landing. Then Hawk slipped along the hardwood hallway until he reached the door he needed. He paused, listening. A woman's voice could be heard to say, "Please, not again."

The voice was English. Hawk's heart raced. Could he have gotten lucky to find Polly White be on the other side of the door with the target?

"You'll do as I say or I'll tell Damyan."

"But—"

"No buts. Roll over. We're doing it again."

"But it hurts."

Hawk heard the slap of palm on skin. That was enough. He tried the handle and found it locked. His foot came up and crashed against the door near the lock. Wood splintered and the door crashed back.

His forced entry was met with yelps of surprise from the two naked people on the king-sized bed situated overlooking the Black Sea through floor to ceiling, double-glazed window.

"What—who are you?" Marinov spluttered.

"Shut the fuck up," Hawk hissed. He turned his attention to the girl. She had bruises on her face and dark rings around her eyes. The Talon operator touched his own face and asked, "Did he do that, lass?"

"You're English?"

Ignoring the comment, he repeated his question, "Did he do that to your face?"

"N—No. Are you here to help me?" she asked trying to cover herself with the sheet.

"You can't do this," Marinov said in high-pitched English.

Hawk shot him in the leg. "You were frigging warned, mate."

Marinov cried out in pain, but Hawk ignored him. "What is your name, girl?"

"Mary. Mary Hollister."

"Shit," Hawk hissed. "It couldn't be that easy, could it."

"Are you here to take me home?"

"Sure, girl, sure. Do you have any clothes?"

"Yes."

"Put them on and wait out in the hallway. Tell me if anyone comes along."

She slid off the bed and Hawk noticed the other bruises on her body. "How long have you been here, Mary?"

"I don't know."

"Alpha Two, copy?"

"Copy, Jake."

"Dig up what you can on a Mary Hollister, age—how old are you, Mary?"

"Twenty."

"Age twenty."

"Roger that."

Once Mary was dressed, she moved out into the hallway and Hawk turned his attention to the whimpering Marinov who was desperately trying to stop the blood leaking from his leg. "Now, you start talking or the next bullet will be in your guts. I've no time to fuck around. Where is Dragov?"

"I don't know."

Hawk punched him in the wounded leg. The high-pitched scream that rang throughout the house was akin to those heard in horror films. Next Hawk clipped him in the jaw, knocking him back on the bed. "Let's try again."

"I—I don't know. He left town yesterday and won't be back for a few days."

"Where did he go?"

"To shoot a movie."

"Where?"

"Varna."

"How many girls did he take with him?" Hawk asked.

"Just one."

"Who?"

"I don't know her name."

"Where is she from?"

"I don't know.'

The gun came up.

"Wait! I think she's British."

Hawk had a sinking feeling. "What is her name?"

"I told you, I don't know."

"Was it Polly White?"

"I don't know—maybe."

"Was it?"

"Maybe. I don't know, I don't know!"

"Where does he keep the girls?" Hawk asked.

"On the island."

"What island?"

"Look out the window, you can't miss it."

Hawk glanced through the huge pane of glass and saw what Marinov was referring to. There was a headland further along the Black Sea coast with what appeared to be a bridge connecting the coast with the small island. There he could see buildings topped with orange roofs. Out the front there looked to be a small jetty.

"What is that place?"

"He shoots movies and keep the girls there."

"How many?"

Marinov was confused. "What?"

"How many girls are there?"

"Three, four."

"How many guards?"

"I'm not sure."

Hawk clenched his jaw, trying to fight the rage that was building. "How many?"

"Seven."

The Talon operator leaned down and grabbed a handful of hair. "Get up."

"Ouch! Take it easy. My leg."

"Shut up and listen. You are Dragov's accountant?"

"Y—Yes." His voice was hesitant.

"Where do you keep your records?"

"On my computer in the library downstairs."

The radio Hawk had crackled to life with a voice he couldn't understand. "What did he say?" he asked Marinov.

"He is checking in."

"What happens if they don't all check in?"

"They will look for each other to see if all is well."

"Then we don't have much time."

Hawk started pushing the naked, limping man along in front of him and out into the hallway where Mary waited for him. "Where are you taking him?"

"Downstairs. Follow us."

More calls came over the radio that went unanswered and Hawk figured they had a few minutes before the first of the bodies was found.

Blood from Marinov's wound left a trail on the floor and as they walked into the library and closed the door, the man's leg from thigh down was a mass of red.

Inside the room were walls of books and bookshelves, except for the one, like the bedroom upstairs, that took advantage of the view through a large window.

Hawk pushed him down into the chair behind his desk. He then ripped the cord out from a nearby lamp and bound the accountant's legs to the chair's.

"Now, open the files."

"I can't."

"Yes, you can. I can't because I don't know the password. You do. You're going to open them, get me into his accounts."

"I can't, he'll kill me."

Suddenly Hawk heard footsteps and guessed that one of the guards had finally entered the house. What impressed the Talon operator was that he hadn't called out to see if everything was all right giving himself more chance of catching whoever was there unaware. Too bad he was heavy-footed.

Hawk turned just as the door opened; obviously the guard had heard the voices. The Talon operative fired three times, the bullets punching through the hollow door. A stifled cry of pain was followed by a dull thud as the guard collapsed to the floor.

Hurrying over to pull the door the rest of the way open, Hawk found the guard dead.

Crossing back to the desk, Hawk smacked Marinov up the back of his head. "Get me in now or I'm going to put a bullet in your fucking head."

"Then how will you get what you want?"

"Fine, you had your chance," Hawk growled and as promised, shot him in the head.

He reached into his pocket and took out a thumb drive and put it into the USB port. "Alpha Two, you should be up and running."

"I'll need a couple of minutes, Jake."

"Take your time."

"Is—is he dead?" Mary asked hesitantly.

"As dead as they come."

"I'm pleased. He was an animal. The things he made me do..."

"You don't have to worry about that now. Where are you from?"

"Liverpool."

"I should have guessed. Listen, can you stay here for me? No matter what, don't go anywhere."

"Where are you going?"

"Not far. Alpha Two, where is that last guard?"

"Approaching the rear of the house, Bravo One."

Hawk walked through the house towards the rear where the kitchen was. "He should be inside now, Jake," Ilse said.

The Brit stopped and listened.

"Jake, he's coming towards you. He'll be on top of you in...three...two...one..."

Hawk poked the gun around the doorjamb and squeezed the trigger three times. He heard the audible grunt of surprise and then the final guard fall to the floor. Jake stepped out from where he was and looked down. "Alpha Two, the house is secure. Five X-rays down hard."

"Five?"

"Affirmative, five."

"Copy. The download is almost complete."

"Roger that. Did you dig up anything on Mary Hollister?" he asked as he made his way back towards the library.

"Jake, the only thing I can find on a Mary Hollister is a girl from Liverpool."

"That's the one."

"She disappeared two years ago when she was eighteen. Family holiday in Paris. No sign of her since."

"And she's still alive. That doesn't make sense."

"All I know is what I've got in front of me."

Hawk made his way back through the house towards the library and when he pushed open the door he stopped abruptly. Standing before him was Mary Hollister with a gun pointed right at his chest. "I guess I know the reason why you're still alive."

"I knew it was only a matter of time. No one stays on the inside like I have, unless they're someone special."

"What's so special about you?"

"Damyan likes me. He treats me special."

"If you call them bruises over your body special, then you've got it made, kid. What happened? Did you fall in love with him?"

"Yes. He loves me, too. Even more, if I kill you."

Hawk shrugged. "You keep telling yourself that maybe one day you'll believe it."

"Jake, what's going on?" Ilse asked.

He said, "It looks like I've worked out why she's still alive, Alpha Two. Looks like we've got a case of Stockholm Syndrome."

"Can you handle it, Jake?"

"I think so. Give me a moment."

"Don't come any closer," she hissed. "I'll shoot."

"I thought that's what you were going to do anyway," Hawk replied.

Mary hesitated.

"You do know what he does, don't you?"

"He makes pornographic movies."

"That's right. But not just ordinary movies."

"Of course they are. I've been in one with him. He cares about me."

"If he cares about you, why are you here screwing Marinov?"

"Because he asked me to."

"It didn't sound like you were enjoying it much."

"It's a sacrifice he asked me to make."

Hawk stepped forward. "I'll be stuffed, girl, listen to yourself. He's got you so brainwashed that you'll do anything for him. Shit, the movies he makes, what happens to the girls after?"

"They go home."

The Talon operator couldn't believe what he was hearing. He shook his head. "No, they don't. They get right to the end of the movie and as they are faking their last orgasm, some fucker cuts their fucking throats. It's called a snuff movie."

Her eyes widened. "You lie!"

"Am I? Listen to yourself. The guy beats you, hence all the bruises. He gives you to people like Marinov to sleep with, and I bet he has you hooked on drugs as well."

Mary's expression changed to one of anxiety. Tears welled in her eyes. "It's not true. He loves me."

"Hell, girl, your parents love you. Dragov, on the other hand, he'll wake up one morning and decide to put you in one of his movies again. Only this time he'll kill you. You're better off coming with me."

"*Lies!*" she screamed. "All lies."

"I wish it was, girl."

Suddenly her shoulders slumped, and her demeanor changed dramatically. She lowered the weapon and it seemed as though the devastation she felt was complete. Hawk stepped forward and was about to take the weapon from her when it came up through ninety degrees and kept rising until it was pressed firmly under her chin.

"No!" Hawk shouted but it was all to no avail. The gun fired and she fell to the floor in a crumpled heap. "Shit, girl, why did you go and do that?"

"Jake, what happened?" Ilse asked over his comms.

"Nothing. Are you done? I'm coming out."

"Alone?"

"Yeah, alone. Have the boat standing by."

———

IT WAS ALMOST midnight when Hawk emerged from the water and changed silently out of his wetsuit. Out of his waterproof bag he took his NVGs and his comms device. By the time he was ready to move he was kitted out in his gear.

"Alpha Two, comms check, over."

"Read you loud and clear, Bravo One."

"Roger that."

"Be advised you have one X-ray at your ten, approximately twenty meters from your location."

"Copy."

Hawk moved silently up from the shoreline, Heckler and Koch MP5SD in his hands up and ready to fire. Through the green curtain of the NVGs the figure appeared. The laser sight on the weapon settled on the X-ray and Hawk stroked the trigger. A short burst reached out and touched the figure that jerked and fell to the ground.

"X-ray down."

"Jake, ISR shows two more X-rays outside and four more in the main building. I also have two heat signatures inside each of the two smaller buildings."

"They'll be the girls," Hawk said. "I'll secure the outside then the main building before going after them. Keep an eye out on the approaches while I do it."

"Roger that. Your next target is further along the shoreline."

"Copy."

Hawk started moving low following the shoreline until he found the second target. Once again, the MP5 spat, and the man went down.

"Jake, at your three, approximately one-hundred meters is the third outriding X-ray."

"Copy."

Hawk changed direction, putting the first of the smaller buildings between himself and the target he was stalking.

"Bravo, the X-ray is walking in your direction."

"Copy," Hawk replied and took cover behind the building, resting his shoulder against the rough stone exterior.

"Jake, I have movement from the main building."

"Bollocks. What's our X-ray doing?"

"Still coming your way."

"Roger."

Hawk circled around the building to get in behind the

guard. Moments later, he came up behind him, his combat knife in his right hand. The Talon operator's left hand came up and clamped over the guard's mouth. The knife-filled hand came around and plunged violently into the guard's chest twice.

The man's body stiffened with shock and Hawk felt the alarmed shout die as the expelled breath was muffled by his hand. The knife then slashed across the already dying man's throat making certain there was no coming back.

But the guard had one last protest up his sleeve. His finger had been on the trigger and with a dying reflex, it tightened, releasing a long burst.

"Fucking hell," Hawk growled as bullets howled into the night.

He put his knife away and grabbed the MP5 which had been hanging by a strap. "Alpha Two, things are about to go loud. I've been rumbled. I'm moving to the bridge."

"Copy, Bravo."

Hawk turned and started for the bridge that connected the mainland with the island. Once there he dropped the backpack he was wearing and opened it. He was now glad that he had brought it just in case.

"Bravo One, we've just intercepted a call from the island to the local police. They're starting to move and may be about five minutes out."

"Roger that," he responded as he took out the explosive brick of C-4.

"Jake, the remaining X-rays are starting a search."

"Copy."

Hawk kept about his business as he put the explosive in place, rigging it to detonate.

"Jake, the police are two minutes out."

Finishing up, he returned to his pack where he'd left the trigger; picking it up, he detonated the C-4.

An orange flash lit up the night as the illuminated

mushroom cloud rose towards the stars. "Alpha Two, get the boat in here now."

"Roger."

Hawk caught movement back towards the buildings and brought up the MP5. He waited while the figure came closer and then fired.

"X-ray down. Moving to the first building."

He pushed forward cautiously until he reached the target building. As he slipped around the front, another guard appeared. Hawk fired and then the count was one less. "Where are the other two bastards?"

"Moving down the left side of the island."

Hawk tried the door but found it locked. Using his boot, he kicked it open, sending the door flying back on its hinges until it crashed against the wall. He stepped inside.

Two young women were huddled together in the corner, trembling with fear. "It's all right, I'm here to get you out."

One of them babbled something in German. Hawk quickly changed his dialect and repeated what he'd just said.

"You are here to help us?"

"Yes. You have to come with me."

"We cannot leave. The guards."

"Leave them to me. But if you don't come with me now, I'll leave you behind."

"No! We'll come." The young lady spoke to her friend and they both got to their feet.

Hawk said into his comms. "Alpha Two. Copy?"

"Copy."

"I have two packages secure. Moving to the next location."

"Copy. You have two packages secure."

He turned to the girls and said, "Follow me."

Hawk led them out into the night and started towards the second of the two smaller outbuildings.

"Jake, be aware that the police have arrived at the bridge."

"Where's the boat?"

"Three mikes out."

"Roger."

He'd only taken a couple more steps when Ilse's urgent voice came over the comms. "Hold, Bravo. X-rays are coming your way."

Hawk went down onto his knee. He turned to the girls. "Get down."

They lay flat on the damp grass trying their best to keep out of sight, still shaking with fear. The former SAS man swept the ground before him and then picked up his targets as they appeared from behind the building he was headed for, flashlights shining.

The MP5 came up to his shoulder and once the laser sights came on, he opened fire. He heard the cries of anguish as both men fell, writhing on the ground. He said to the girls, "Get the others from in there. I'll be with you in a moment."

He hurried across to the fallen men and took out his SIG, shooting them both to make sure they stayed down.

He rejoined the girls who were all babbling anxiously about what was happening. "Keep it down and follow me," he said to them.

"You're English," came an unmistakably accented voice.

Could it be? "What's your name, girl?"

"Louise Shaw. Thank you, thank you, thank you."

"Quiet down. Polly White, do you know her?"

"Polly?"

"Yes."

"Damyan took her and Rose with him."

He took two. "Christ. Alpha One, I've now secured four packages. The HVT is not here, I repeat, the HVT is not here. Moving to extract."

174

"Roger, Bravo. You might want to pick it up, it looks like the police have found a way to cross to the island on foot."

"Yeah, well I won't be here when they arrive." He looked at the girls. "Come on, you're going home."

CHAPTER FIFTEEN

Berlin, Germany

"JUST WHAT I wanted to do on a rainy night," Mac MacBride growled. "Search and clear a fucking rundown machinery factory. I bet it's got damn holes in the roof and all."

The team's designated marksman, Nemo Kent, looked at his friend in the blacked-out Mercedes Benz van and said, "Getting soft, are we?"

"Fuck you."

"All right, you lot, game faces on," said Grizz Harvey.

The rear door opened, and a gust of cold damp air rushed in past Karl. "Close the frigging door," Mac growled.

Karl sat down next to Harvey and opened his laptop. After a few moments of tapping keys, he had all his links up and working. "Okay, everybody get their comms set."

He waited a few moments while Harvey's team got ready. The team leader said, "We all good?"

"I'm up," Nemo replied.

"Me, too," said Mac.

"Linc?"

Linc Sheffield was a big man like Harvey as well as his second in command. "Yeah, I'm good."

"Great," Karl said. "Listen, there are at least eight targets inside the factory. As you were briefed, they are under the command of Pavli Jasari. The ID was made when we received anonymous intel. Nearly all the people he has working for him are former military. They are dangerous and cunning, so when you breach just be aware that there could be boobytraps, tripwires, anything."

"How are we going to play this, Grizz?" asked Nemo.

"We're going in the front door and we'll clean them out. Nothing fancy, just straight up hit and kill."

Linc nodded. "Sounds like a plan to me. Let's do it."

The four operators jumped down from the van into the cold, damp night. The rain had eased to a light mist, but puddles were everywhere. With his CZ Bren2 up at his shoulder, Harvey led the team towards the factory.

Through his night vision goggles, he saw the first guard standing under shelter next to the entry point they planned on using. He squeezed the trigger on the Bren and a THWAP reached his ears. The guard dropped like a stone, spilling out into the mist.

MacBride reached out and tried the handle of the door which would let them into the factory. It was unlocked and he pushed it open just far enough to allow him and the rest of the team to slip through.

Inside it was dark and damp, MacBride having been correct in his assumption about there being holes in the roof everywhere, and large drips seemed to fall from each opening like they were in a metal rainforest.

Outside, using the ISR from the van Karl monitored their progress. His voice came over the comms, "Proceed directly ahead. You will reach a door; beyond that door you will find another room. In that room on the right there will be some stairs. You need to go up them to the second level."

"Copy," Harvey whispered. "Linc, on point."

Linc led them across the room, their boots splashing through small puddles as they went until they finally reached the doorway. He tried the door and found it unlocked.

The inside room was full of old machinery lined up in rows. He moved to his right, each open alleyway he passed, his weapon swept it to make sure it was clear.

At the bottom of the stairs, he waited for the rest of the team before starting to ascend. As he lifted his right foot to place it on the first step, a hand clamped down on his shoulder, stopping him immediately.

"Are you trying to get us killed?" Harvey asked as he whispered in his ear. "Look the fuck down next time."

The tripwire was crude, but effective. A grenade on one side with a thin filament attached to the pin and then tied off on the other side of the stairs. Harvey took a pair of cutters out of his pocket and leant down to snip the filament. Once the trip wire was cut, it was safer for them to continue their mission.

When they reached the top of the stairs, Karl said, "On the north side of the building is another room. The rest of the heat signatures are emanating from there."

Harvey tapped Linc on his shoulder. The operator moved forward then after five steps stopped cold. "Motherfucker."

"What is it?" asked Harvey?

Before the question could be answered, Karl's voice came back over the comms. "I don't know what you've done, but we've got movement. I'm picking up a signal, too. You didn't happen to trip a motion sensor by any chance?"

Harvey knew exactly that's what had happened. He said, "Split up and keep low. We're about to have contact."

Sudden gunfire erupted, filling the room with a continuous roar. Harvey and his men dove for cover behind old rusting metal shelving units. Bullets howled as they ricocheted off the solid steel frames.

"Talk to me, Karl, what do you see?" Harvey asked.

"They're splitting up, coming down either side. They're trying to flank you."

Harvey took a fragmentation grenade from his webbing, pulled the pin and tossed it to the right side of the room. "Frag out!"

An orange flesh was followed by a deafening roar as the grenade detonated. What was left of the windows on that side of the room disintegrated as the blast smashed the glass sending it flying outward. Into his comms, Harvey said, "Nemo, Mac, push right, push, right."

With Linc following him, Harvey moved along the left-hand side of the building. A figure loomed out of the green haze before him. The Bren in his hands came to life and the figure cried out as a burst of gunfire punched into his chest.

The shooting inside the factory intensified forcing Harvey and Linc to take cover behind a large steel box. Bullets pinged off it and ricocheted in every direction. "Shit," Harvey hissed.

"Who'd have thought they would have motion sensors?" Linc growled.

"You should have," Harvey snapped. "Nemo, we're pinned down over this side."

Harvey heard Nemo say, "Be right with you, Grizz."

Bullets kept hammering the box and screaming off into the darkness. Harvey looked at the object they were sheltered behind and said, "I don't know what this is but I'm glad it is made of steel." He then fired at the flashes until his magazine ran dry, then he reloaded the Bren.

Suddenly to their front he heard a shout and then another explosion rocked the factory. Harvey and Linc ducked down behind their cover as what were left of the windows blew out.

Moments later, a call came across their net. "Clear! All targets down."

Berlin, Germany

"One fucking step behind all of the time!" Hawk snarled.

Anja nodded. "Overall, a good result, Jake. You saved four girls from almost certain death."

"Yeah, but not the right one."

"I'm sure their parents wouldn't agree with you on that. Interpol scrambled to the address we gave them from all the intel gained from the computer, but Damyan wasn't there, nor were the girls. But in saying that, they were also able to raid the brothels that he owned and scooped up more, putting him out of business."

"But he's still out there."

"We'll find him. On a brighter note, Mister Harvey managed to solve our Albanian issue."

"That's something, I guess."

"How are you feeling?"

"Fine."

"You look tired. Get some rest."

"Not yet. I need to help find Dragov."

Anja reached out and touched his hand. "The others are doing it. Get rested. I can't have my best man falling asleep at the wheel, so to speak."

He sighed. "Yes, ma'am."

Ilse appeared at the door. "We have a problem."

TO SAY that the problem was big was a gross understatement. Quite frankly, Anja had never even heard of something like it happening before. "Two Polly Whites?"

"Yes, ma'am." The two pictures flashed up onto the screen. "Two of them."

Hawk stared at them. Both had dark hair, brown eyes, and that was about as far as the likenesses went. "Bollocks, someone sure fucked up."

"Get Mary Thurston on the line," Anja snapped. "How are we only just finding this out now? Surely this should have come to light well before now."

"One of the prisoners that Jake brought back, the English girl, said that Polly often talked about her home in Surrey."

"But Polly White doesn't live in Surrey."

"Exactly. So then I had Karl dive back into it. A second Polly White disappeared the same time that our Polly White did."

"So Medusa fucked up," Hawk said. "Erkens fucked up. They took the wrong one. I need to speak to him."

"Slow down for a moment; let's work the problem," Anja said. "Erkens grabs the wrong girl and—"

"No," said Hawk. "I remember now, Federov said his people grabbed her. They just passed her on through the chain until she reached Osman."

"But Osman gets his ransom and instead of killing the girl, he sells her on."

"But why not kill her?" Ilse asked. "He got what he wanted."

"He found out," Hawk said. "Somehow he found out he had the wrong Polly White."

"But then he just kills her, surely," Ilse said. "He got paid."

Anja held up her hand. "No, wait, we're missing something."

"What?" Hawk asked.

"We have two Polly Whites that went missing at the same time."

"Wait," said Hawk. "We assume they went missing at the same time."

With a nod, Anja continued. "Let's assume that Polly One is the one that goes to Osman. Somehow, he finds out that she is the wrong one and he knows that when he demands the ransom, which upon wanting proof of life they will see that it's not her. What do you do?"

"Sell her as *the* Polly White to the highest bidder."

"Which happens to be Dasan Ansari who pays Osman and then sells her to Damyan Dragov, neither man any the wiser that this Polly White is an imposter," Anja theorized.

"Oh bollocks," Hawk growled. "The fucking prick knew."

Both women looked at Hawk. He said, "George White. He knew we were following the wrong trail. There was no ransom, he just said there was. Whoever has Polly White is a big fish and they're using her against her father to get whatever they need from him."

Ilse said, "Well, he is the Foreign Secretary."

"The thing is, what do they want?"

Anja said, "The only people who will know are MI6 and MI5."

Karl appeared, a solemn expression on his face. "I've just been informed by Interpol that they've recovered Polly White and Rose Larson."

"Recovered?" asked Hawk.

He nodded.

"Fuck."

"There was something else. A recording."

"Of what?" Hawk asked.

Karl just stared at him until the penny dropped. "Bloody hell."

"They believe it was going to be posted all across the

internet to show—" He shook his head. "I don't know. They're fucking sick."

"Is there any lead on Dragov?"

Karl shook his head and cleared his throat. "No, nothing."

Anja nodded. "Meanwhile, everybody gather your things. We're going to Britain. There are some people there I need to see."

The meeting broke up, but Anja held Hawk back. "Don't blame yourself for this, Jake. We did our best."

"Yeah, but it wasn't bloody good enough, was it?"

"You still managed to save some girls, take that as a win. You should know as a special operator that not every mission works out. We'll go to Hereford and regroup while we try to figure out our next move."

"I already know our next move, boss, it's go after that sadistic fucker and burn down his fucking house before he sets up another."

"Don't forget we still have another girl in play."

"I haven't but you're forgetting that no one wants us to take the field on that one."

"We'll see."

"Yes, we will."

Anja thought for a moment. "Viktor Medvedev is dead."

Hawk froze. "What?"

"It looks like he was killed by one of his own."

"Noskov?"

"Possibly. However, if it was him, he's gone to ground. My guess is he's taken over and put Medusa back in the shadows. Which also means we were getting too close."

"Then we'll just have to draw him out."

"We will. By going to war with every sex trafficker across the globe. We shut them down and he doesn't have a business. He'll have to surface eventually to stop us. Now, go and get ready, we're wheels up in an hour."

CHAPTER SIXTEEN

MI5, London

ANJA MEYER and Mary Thurston sat across from Frank Fitzgerald waiting patiently to hear his explanation as to what was going on. Nothing on the topic was forthcoming, especially since he was waiting for the arrival of the Foreign Secretary.

The man appeared to be somewhere between fifty and sixty, maybe even slightly older. It was hard to pinpoint his age exactly. His face remained passive throughout the staring contest across his polished-top desk.

Thurston's patience was worn through and she was done waiting. "Did you know about this?"

"The security services were informed, yes."

"Shit, Frank. You could have let us fucking know."

"Wasn't my call, Mary."

"Then, whose call was it?"

The door opened and a tall, thin, gray-haired man entered wearing a suit. He looked around the room before sitting down. "Alright, I'm here now."

Anja stared at him, her eyes cold. "Are you George White?"

"I am. Who are you?"

"I'm the woman who's been trying to find your daughter. Except the girl we were trying to find wasn't even her, was she?"

"I have nothing to say on the matter."

"You arrogant pompous asshole," Anja hissed. "I have my people put in danger trying to find this girl. And you knew all the time it wasn't her."

"Would it have changed anything?" White asked.

"Not a damn thing. But it would have been nice to know."

He looked at Thurston. "My missing daughter has nothing to do with you. You and your mercenaries stay away from it before you ruin everything."

Thurston leaned forward in her seat. "They are not my team. They are her team. And at this point in time, they're about the only chance you have of getting your daughter back in one piece."

"What do they want?" Anja asked.

"It is nothing to do with you."

"You're the British Foreign Secretary, I'm thinking there's a lot that they want from you. Something you can't give them. At this point you are playing for time. Either that or you've given up hope and consider your daughter already dead. Which one is it?"

White abruptly came to his feet. "I don't have to listen to this."

Anja produced an envelope and withdrew a photograph from within. She slammed it on the desk and poked her straightened finger at it. "This is Polly White. The *other* Polly White. The one who was mistaken for your daughter. Her parents were told this morning that she is dead. That comes back on you."

185

White gave her an indignant look. "It has nothing to do with me."

"Oh yes, it has. You were the one that ordered the strike which killed Mustafa Osman's wife. In fact, she was the target. But she got killed. So Mustafa Osman targeted your daughter. But it all got fucked up and they grabbed the wrong Polly White. So yes, it is your fault."

"We needed leverage to get him," White said.

"She was a woman."

"She was a damn terrorist," he spat back at her.

"How was she? She wasn't even on the terrorist watch list."

"Guilty by association."

"You're an idiot. Who has your daughter?"

"It doesn't matter. We don't negotiate with terrorists."

Anja tensed. "So you're not even going to try? You're just going to leave your daughter out there to die at the hands of whoever. Give me a name. My team and I will get her back for you."

"If you know what's good for you, you will stay away," White growled.

"What are you hiding, Mr. White?" Thurston asked.

"You don't need to know."

The foreign secretary turned and stomped out of the room.

Anja looked at the head of MI5. "Can you help us with anything?"

"The man told you to leave it."

"The same man that just ordered us to let his daughter die."

Fitzgerald got up from his seat and walked over to the blinds that covered his glass fishbowl office. He closed each one in turn before returning to his chair. Then tapping on his keyboard, he brought something up on his computer monitor.

He twisted it so they could see, then hit play to start

the video that was there. When the picture came into view both women could see that the bound and gagged person was Polly White. The camera angle changed, and a masked man came into view holding up a newspaper. Then came the words. "We have your daughter. We're willing to exchange her for the list. Your move."

That was it, nothing more.

"Who are they?" Anja asked.

"We don't know."

"I heard an accent. Asian?"

"It is quite possible that they could be."

"What is the list, Mr. Fitzgerald?"

The intelligence service boss remained silent.

"Mr. Fitzgerald, if my team and myself are to get this girl back we need to know everything. What is the list?"

"Over the past few years, the intelligence services MI5 and MI6 have been putting together a list. That list is of known agents or operatives—whichever you want to call them—operating across Europe in different countries."

"British?" Thurston queried.

Fitzgerald shook his head. "Not just British. American, German, Israeli, even ones from NATO. Somehow, whoever has this girl found out about it and now they want it."

Anja was astounded by the news. "A list like that in the wrong hands could not only cripple every nation's intelligence services, but it would set relations back by 100 years."

"Which is why we're not handing it over."

"And that is why you need us."

"This is an intelligence services matter. It's nothing to do with people trafficking and abductions," Fitzgerald pointed out.

"You seem to be forgetting one thing, Mr. Fitzgerald," Anja pointed out.

"What is that?"

"Finding abducted girls like Polly White is what we do. It is the purview of our team."

Fitzgerald thought about it long and hard before answering. "Let me take it up the chain to the Home Office. I'll talk to the Home Secretary about it before I give you anything."

Anja nodded. "How long will that take?"

"A day or two."

"You do realize she could be dead by then."

The MI5 boss's face remained sober. "Quite frankly, Miss Meyer. I'd be surprised if she's still alive even now. I think you're trying to find a corpse."

"One more thing. I'm assuming she wasn't taken from Brussels. Where?"

"Paris."

Once they were outside the building, Thurston said, "Did you see the date on that newspaper?"

Anja nodded. "Yes. She was taken after Polly One."

"Which means?"

"Which means everything we've been told is a lie."

———

"I AGREE WITH HIM," said Hawk. "The foreign secretary hasn't given them what they want. They would have killed her and moved on by now."

"But what if they haven't? What if they still have her?" asked Ilse.

Hawk looked at her. "Why? Why would they keep her alive after all this time? Especially when it's obvious they're not going to get what they want."

Anja said, "We have to take everything we've been told so far about Polly White and consider it to be a lie. We start from square one."

"We're going all the way back to the start?" Hawk groaned.

"Yes," Anja replied. "Which is why you're coming with me."

"Where are we going?"

"To see an old friend."

———

MI6 Secure Facility, Europe

Federov smiled. "Two visitors in one day, I must be popular."

"Shut up, Leonid," Hawk growled. "Just listen."

"Fine, I'm listening. What is so important that two of you need to come and see me."

"First things first," Anja said. "Your boss is dead."

The Russian's face remained passive.

"Bloody hell," snapped Hawk. "You already fucking knew."

Federov shrugged. "I hear things in here. I'm guessing it was Ilya Noskov who did it. However, I bet he's disappeared now, and you've come to me to see if I have any ideas where he might be. Well, I don't so you've wasted your time."

"That's where you're wrong, Leonid," Anja said. "We're here on other matters."

"Yes?"

"Your people screwed up when they grabbed Polly White," Hawk told him. "They grabbed the wrong person."

"Impossible. They grabbed Polly White. She had identification on her."

"There were two Polly Whites, you dumb prick. The one your people grabbed was from Surrey."

"Oh, dear."

Hawk's fist crashed against his jaw.

"What was that for?"

"For being you, shithead. An innocent girl died because of you."

He was about to say that it wasn't his fault but stopped for he knew if he said that, Hawk would hit him again.

"As it was," said Anja, "someone else took her. After the first Polly was taken."

Federov remained silent.

"What do you know about a list that the British had with intelligence agents on it?"

"I may have heard something a while back. Travelling like we did you hear things."

"What would something like that be worth?" Hawk asked.

"It depends. Maybe fifty to one-hundred million."

Hawk's eyes narrowed. "Think very carefully before you answer this. Did you hear of anyone who was planning to make a play for it?"

"Maybe."

"Who has the skills to pull something like this off?"

"Outside of Medusa, any number of foreign intelligence agencies."

Hawk was becoming frustrated. "I know that. But which frigging one?"

"Section Three."

Hawk came across the table and grabbed Federov by the shirt. "You lying—"

"It's true! It's true!"

"There is no Section Three, asshole."

"There is, I'm telling you. They're North Korean."

Hawk let him go and thrust him back into his seat. He glanced at Anja who remained silent. "Do you know anything about this?"

"Only whispers. That's what German Intelligence thought they were. At first."

"Then somebody better catch me up."

"Rumor had it that Section Three was formed by the

190

North Koreans as an intelligence gathering operation. It was unique because the North Koreans set up a string of high-class escort services in major cities. It's amazing how many men, when away from home for an extended period of time, get lonely. Straight away it started to pay dividends for them. Soon Section Three was raking in intelligence across the globe at an embarrassing rate. Eventually British, German, and US intelligence formulated a plan to dismantle their network. The operation was a success."

"Obviously not," Hawk replied.

"It is quite possible that they have set up a new network."

"They have," Federov said with a nod. "Medusa was asked to supply some of the girls for it."

"Of course they were," Hawk growled.

"How long ago did they reappear?"

"Two years."

"Where have they set up?" Hawk asked.

"Berlin, London, Paris, New York, and a hundred other places."

Anja stared at him. "Who in Paris could have taken her?"

"You're wasting your time; she won't be there."

"But whoever took her will be. Who was it?"

"Henri Chaplin. He is a retrieval expert. We've used him a few times when we needed something specific."

"We?" Hawk asked knowing what the answer would be.

"Medusa."

"In other words, he's an abduction expert," Anja said.

"If you say so."

Hawk looked at Anja. "What do you think?"

"We make Henri Chaplin our target."

"My thoughts exactly."

"Your information confirms most of what we know," said Frank Fitzgerald. "I talked with the Home Secretary. I have been given permission to provide you with any assistance you need."

"We need a location on Henri Chaplin," Anja said.

"Who is Henri Chaplin?"

"He was the scouser who took Polly White," Hawk said. "I'm guessing that is something that you didn't know."

"Where did you get the information from?"

"Our source in Europe."

"Fedorov?"

"The one and only. You know, he has come in quite handy since we've had him on ice. Turns out, Medusa has used Chaplin before. They refer to him as an extraction specialist. It's just a fancy name for an abductor or kidnapper. Federov said to find him. Odds are that he is the one most likely responsible for having taken her from Paris."

"I will see what my people can come up with. However, I can't promise anything."

"Just a location. That's all we need. We'll take care of the rest ourselves."

Fitzgerald sighed. "I was hoping that Section Three were gone forever. I guess it was too much to wish for. At least now that we know they're back, we can set up operations to find and track them. Is there anything else?"

Anja shook her head. "No, that'll be it for the time being."

"One thing before you go. You, your team, you all do good work. You have accomplished more in the short time you've been doing this than any other organization over the past few years. I'm starting to think that Thurston and Hank Jones have done a good thing. I wish you luck. And if ever in the future you need help to do what you're doing, reach out, I'll be here."

"Thank you."

———

"That didn't take long," Ilse said as she sat down opposite Hawk "MI5 came through already."

"Where is he?"

"We don't have an exact fix on him, but they gave us a few locations that might prove useful; at least it gives us a place to start."

"Do we have a picture of what he looks like?"

Ilse opened a folder with papers in it. She dug through them until she found a photo. Hawk frowned. "How do you get so much information so quick?"

"It's called practice. And experience." She passed the photo over to him.

Chaplin was a thin faced man with a hawkish nose. He had dark hair and looked to be somewhere in his mid-40s. Hawk guessed that he had his hair colored to cover any gray that might be showing. Ilse passed another sheet of paper to him. This one gave the man's specs.

She said, "Henri Chaplin is in his mid-40s. He is a native of Paris, but he travels widely through Europe itself. He once served in the Foreign Legion, but now he's up for hire to the highest bidder. His specialty, as you know, is extraction. He doesn't work alone. He works with a team of at least three, maybe four people."

"It takes a team to kidnap someone," the former SAS man said.

"When he's in Paris, he's a creature of habit. He visits the same cafes, the same restaurants. And drives the same route to each."

"You would think a man of his profession would learn not to be so predictable."

"Or he's just overconfident," Ilse replied.

"Which one do we stakeout? The cafes or the restaurants?"

Ilse grinned. "Definitely the restaurants."

Hawk was curious. "Why them?"

"It seems our friend Chaplin considers himself a bit of a ladies' man. With honey we shall catch."

"Alright, I have a question that I figure needs to be answered. Why haven't Interpol or any other law system taken him off the board?"

"Because he's good at what he does. He has never been caught with his victim. Or left any trace behind that will link them or himself to the crime."

"So, in fact we know he does it. But we can't prove he does it."

"Nothing that will stand up in a court of law."

"Can I kill him?"

"No, you can't kill him, Jacob." It was Anja.

"It would save a lot of pain and angst."

"We will record whatever we get out of him and then we will turn him over to Interpol where they will use that recording against him."

"I still think shooting him is the easier option."

"I'm sure you do."

"What is the plan?" asked Hawk.

"Ilse will be our bait. We will put her in play and see if she can reel our man in."

Hawk nodded. "That's all well and good. But first we have to make sure that he's going to be in the place where we want him to be."

"I agree. That's why Ilse has lost her dog."

The former SAS man chuckled. "Lost her dog? You're going with that?"

"While out jogging, of course."

"Oh, yes? I suppose with very little on?"

"Just enough to hook our fish and make him squirm."

—————

Paris, France

Hawk sat in the back of the white Mercedes Benz van and watched Ilse get out of her tracksuit. Beneath it she wore a small sports top which accentuated her breast size and showed off her ripped midsection. Then there were the skintight running pants. She grinned at him, aware he was having trouble taking his eyes off her. "Do you like what you see?" she teased.

The Brit went red. "Maybe I should have stayed in the front."

"Never mind, almost done."

She reached out and took the bottle of water he was holding. But instead of drinking it, she poured some of it over her chest and then her face to look as though she'd just been running a marathon.

Replacing the lid, she asked Hawk, "How do I look?"

"H—"

"If you say hot, I'm going to throw the bottle at you."

"I was going to say like you've been running for a long time."

She looked at him skeptically before putting the bottle down, climbing out of the van and closing the door. Hawk let out a long breath. "And fucking hot."

"I can hear you."

He winced.

Outside Ilse grinned and adjusted her earwig. Then she jogged across the street toward the terraced houses and onto the sidewalk where she climbed the steps to the blue door and rang the doorbell.

"Yes?" a man's voice asked in French.

"I wonder if you could help me?" Ilse replied in the man's native tongue.

"Help you with what?"

"I was out running—" Suddenly something occurred to Ilse. "I'm looking for my friend."

Hawk frowned. Then he realized what she was doing. There was no way he would believe that she had lost her dog. Not living where he was. So Ilse had changed the plan on the fly.

"What is your friend's name?"

"Vivian."

"There is no Vivian that lives here."

"Are you sure?"

"I just said so, didn't I?"

"Is this number 14?"

"Yes, it is."

"Is this number 14?" She asked, repeating the question.

"Yes, it is."

"I'm sorry, what was that?" Ilse asked.

"I said yes, it is." There was frustration in the man's voice.

"I'm sorry I can't quite hear you."

"Wait, I will be there shortly."

"Smart girl," Hawk said.

"I was born with it."

The door opened and Chaplin stood before her. He paused, his eyes widening a touch as he looked her up and down. They lingered on her breasts for a few moments before going back to her face. "I said yes, this is number 14."

"And Vivian doesn't live here?"

He shook his head. "No. Just me. All alone."

Ilse pouted at him. "That is sad. I find that if I don't have company, I get lonely."

"You are married?"

Ilse chuckled. "No, no. I'm single. But I have my cat for company."

Now Chaplin was paying closer attention. "It must be a one-sided conversation."

"It can be boring sometimes. I tend to seek out human interaction every so often."

His eyes swept over her once more. "How do you feel about some human interaction?"

"Depends on what you mean?" Ilse replied coyly.

"Dinner. Tonight."

"I—"

"Please?"

She smiled and seemingly relaxed. "All right. Dinner it is. Seven? Eight?"

"Let's make it eight. Wait here."

He disappeared back inside.

"I guess you hooked your fish," Hawk said.

"He wriggles like a small one."

"Just remember he's not."

A couple of minutes later, Chaplin reappeared. Ilse opened her mouth to speak but the gun he held in his fist stopped her. Her blood ran cold, and she said, "What is with the gun?"

————

"FUCKING BOLLOCKS!" Hawk exclaimed as he grabbed his SIG.

He lunged for the van door and threw it open, leaping to the street. Suddenly Hawk stopped. "Fuck a duck. Not again."

Standing before him were three armed men, guns pointed it in his direction. Right off he knew they'd been rumbled. Then as he was about to say something, the lights went out.

CHAPTER SEVENTEEN

Paris, France

"SPEAK TO ME, tell me what happened," Anja snapped.

"Chaplin must have suspected something. As far as I can tell they've been taken by him," Karl explained.

"Get Mister Harvey and his team up," she ordered. "And find me something."

"Doing my best, ma'am."

Anja stood there looking at the big screen they'd had set up. As they watched, the screen went from black to gray as a time stamp showed in the top right corner. Karl said, "I found a camera across the street. I was able to hack into it."

They both peered at the grainy feed. They saw Ilse arrive, start talking to Chaplin, and then saw him go back inside. A couple of minutes later, he reappeared with a gun in his hand. Seconds later, they disappeared inside, and the door closed.

"Could they still be inside?" Anja asked.

Before Karl could answer, four men appeared with

Hawk. Two were holding him up but his feet were dragging across the hard surface of the street. They, too, disappeared inside. "Harvey and his team are mobile, ma'am," Karl said.

Anja nodded. Her eyes remained fixed on the screen as she tried to pick up anything that might help them. "Tell him they're possibly still inside. But hold back once he arrives."

"Yes, ma'am."

"Run that feed back again please, Karl."

He ran the feed and as the men carrying Hawk across the street passed over, she said, "Stop."

Karl could see what she was looking at. One of the men had turned slightly and his face was caught by the camera.

"See if you can get some facial recognition off that guy."

The intelligence analyst's fingers danced across the keyboard. A square appeared around the man's face and within moments it was magnified before the graininess started to clear.

"Good work. Now find out who he is."

The scanner started flicking through face after face after face. Anja stared at it, waiting for the flickering to stop. "What database are you using?"

"Just running it through Interpol at the moment; if I need to, I'll widen it."

"Copy. See if you can find another camera on that street. Maybe we'll get lucky on the other faces," Anja suggested.

"Already looking, ma'am."

And his eyes went back to the facial recognition program as it flicked through like the animated corners on a book.

"I found another camera, ma'am."

The screen split and another picture came up. "This

one is further along the street. It's mounted on a streetlamp."

From this angle, she could see the van and the rest of the street and Ilse as she walked up onto the steps. Once again, they went through the tedium of watching her and Chaplin with their conversation.

Suddenly three terraces down from the one where Ilse was talking to the target, four men emerged from an alley and hurried across the street. Trying to keep out of sight as they moved towards the van. One of them stood beside it while the other three raised their weapons.

Anja and Karl watched as the rear doors flew open and Hawk leapt out before stopping suddenly, realizing that everything was wrong. That was when the man who stood beside the van moved in behind him and struck him down.

"That's how they got Jake," the Talon commander said. "Can we get anything on their faces?"

Karl went back through the feed. His finger hit a button on the keyboard and the feed stopped. A few more taps magnified the picture, and another face appeared through the fog of the screen's pixels.

"I'll put this one into the program as well."

Soon the program was scanning for two men.

Anja's phone buzzed. She hit the button to answer. "Yes?"

"We're two minutes out, ma'am," Harvey said to her.

"There's a possibility that they still could be inside. We haven't seen them come back out. However, there might be a back entrance that we can't see."

"Roger, that. We're changing over to comms now."

Within moments their network was up and running. "Alpha One, this is Eagle One, copy?"

"Roger, Eagle. we're reading you loud and clear."

"Copy. Will make contact once we're there. Out."

"Karl, I want both feeds from the cameras on the

screen so I can see what's going on," Anja said to her analyst.

"Bringing it up now."

Now the screen was split into four. Both cameras and both facial recognition searches.

"Mister Harvey, I want open mics so I can hear what's happening," Anja said.

"Yes, ma'am. ROEs?"

"Rules of engagement are as follows. We need Chaplin alive if possible. Put the others down hard, I don't care about them." Her voice was cold. "I want it contained inside the building. If one of them runs and makes it outside, let them go. Understood?"

"Yes, ma'am."

The SUV they were in swung into view. "We've got you on camera, Mister Harvey, good luck."

The van slowed then stopped. Anja watched on as Harvey and his men climbed out and each one of them had a suppressed handgun out and ready as they crossed the street. Through the open mic, she could hear the heavy breathing. Then they reached the door.

———

HARVEY TOOK A DEEP BREATH. "Right, we don't know what we're going to find on the other side of this door. So have your head on a swivel and be ready for anything."

He reached out and tried the doorknob. It was locked. He glanced along the street both ways and saw that it was clear. The Talon operator turned and tapped Nemo on the shoulder. The team's sniper also doubled as a lock picker. He reached into his pocket and pulled out his little tools. Within seconds of him kneeling in front of it, the door was open.

Harvey went in first, his weapon raised in his hands.

On the other side of the doorway was a small foyer with a staircase going up on the right and a hallway running towards the back of the building on the left. It was all clear and he looked at Linc giving him hand signals to move up the stairs. Mac MacBride followed him as they ascended silently.

Harvey and Nemo Kent walked along the hallway, checking each room as they went. Eventually they ended up in the kitchen at the rear of the small, terraced house. Like the other rooms they checked it was empty, too.

He said into his comms, "We're clear down here."

A few seconds later, Linc said, "We're clear up here, too, Grizz."

"Alpha, we're all clear, no sign of the others or Chaplin. Looks like they went out a rear door."

"Copy, Mr. Harvey. Do a quick check of everything. See if you can find some Intel which might point us in the right direction."

"Roger that."

"Okay, gents, you heard the lady, see what you can find?"

Back in the ops room, Anja turned to Karl. "I need you to find another camera in that backstreet."

"On it right away, ma'am."

It took him couple of minutes, but for a man with Karl's talents, he found one pretty quickly. "I've got one."

One of the live feeds was replaced by a shot from a camera at the rear of the terrorist housing. His fingers danced across the keyboard and within seconds the picture changed. "I don't know why people are so careless with their electronic equipment." There was disdain in his voice.

It was while he was looking for the feed that Anja noticed something that she hadn't noticed before about him. He always started typing with his right hand and he always hit the same key first. The control.

"Why do you do that, Karl?"

"Do what ma'am?" he asked, not looking up.

"Start with the control key first."

"Just my OCD."

"Over the years we worked together before, Karl, I've never noticed that about you."

"I try to hide it."

"Do the others still give you a hard time? About your OCD?"

"No, Miss Meyer. We've actually come to an understanding." He went silent for a moment. Then said, "I have it."

The recorded feed on the camera started playing as they watched the screen. In the street out back, there was a black SUV. At first there was no movement. Then the men with their weapons and Hawk and Ilse appeared. They opened the tailgate and shoved Hawk into the back. Then two of them got in the rear seat with Ilse between them. Chaplin got in the front passenger seat while the third man got in the driver's seat. The SUV pulled away from the curb and sped off.

The fourth man that had been in the film walked out of sight of the camera. Then a minute or so later, a second vehicle appeared. This one looked to be a black Mercedes-Benz. It followed the direction the van took.

Anja said, "Now we know what they're driving, find them. Relay everything that you get to Mr. Harvey."

"Yes, ma'am."

———

HAWK CAME AROUND SLOWLY, remaining silent as he started to make sense of what was happening. The first thing to break through the pain and blackness was the voices. He listened as they spoke French. Male voices occasionally punctuated by a woman's. Ilse.

He lay there rocking with the motion of the vehicle. It came to him that his earwig was gone so the rest of the team wouldn't know where they were. Although he had full confidence they would find them, he wasn't about to wait.

His strength was back after a minute, and after five of them ticked by, he was ready to move.

And he would have if the vehicle hadn't stopped.

Doors opened and people climbed out. The rear door did the same and two men stood pointing handguns at Hawk. He blinked against the brightness of the sun and said, "How's it hanging?"

"Get out," one of them ordered in accented English.

Hawk sat up, his head protesting the move. Ilse appeared with Chaplin standing beside her. "Are you all right, Jake?"

"I'll live," he replied.

"That is a matter of opinion, my friend," Chaplin said. "If you would come with us, the interrogation shall begin."

"Fuck, not again."

"I'm sure the gentlemen will be nice to you, Jake," Ilse said.

"Yeah, right after I discuss the situation with them."

Hawk looked around. They were at what looked to be an old railyard with out-of-service boxcars and carriages scattered throughout. "We catching a train?"

Chaplin nodded. "Most likely the graveyard express."

"Great. I hope it takes in all the scenery."

"Move," snapped one of the other men who was tired of the repartee.

They were guided between two box cars and then across an old, abandoned track before being taken inside a long carriage. "Here will do," Chaplin said.

"What now?" asked Hawk. "You want to do the nice French thing and suck my dick?"

One of the guards hit the former SAS man low in the

kidneys. Hawk stumbled, straightened up, and turned to face the man responsible. "I'm going to break your arm for that."

The man spat at Hawk's feet, his face a study in disdain. Ilse reached out and touched Hawk's arm. "Not yet, Jake, just a little longer."

"Please?"

"Soon, sweetie. We just need to discuss things a little bit longer with Mr. Chaplin. Then you can break the nice man's neck."

"I'll hold you to that."

"If you pair are quite done..."

"What would you like to know, Mr. Chaplin?" Ilse asked.

"Who you are would be a good start."

That Talon Intel officer shrugged. "My name is Ilse Geller, this is Jacob Hawk."

"And why is it that you would target me?"

"Because you're a bloody knob," Hawk stated in a calm voice.

"Now, Jake, play nice."

"Sorry."

"You still haven't answered the question," Chaplin said.

"We received information a short time ago that you are a specialist in a certain field," Ilse explained. "We would like to ask you a few questions about that field."

The Frenchman raised his eyebrows. "Really? What certain field is it that you think I'm in?"

"We were told you were a retrieval expert."

"Fucking kidnapper more like it," Hawk said abrasively.

Ilse rolled her eyes.

"Where did you hear these things? I'm curious." The man's look told a different story; it was somewhere north of idle curiosity.

"Let's just cut to the chase, shall we?" Ilse said. "A few weeks back now a girl was taken from Paris. Her name was Polly White. On information we received, your services are the most likely ones utilized by the person who wanted her."

"I see." Chaplin raised his eyebrows.

"What we are concerned about is the welfare of said girl. We are quite happy to walk away if you can give us the information that will lead to her reacquisition."

Chaplin stared at them both incredulously for several moments before nodding. "All right. I'll admit it, a few weeks back I did pick up a girl from Paris."

Hawk's gaze hardened. "What did you do with her?"

"That is not for you to worry about, my friend."

"Bollocks, it isn't. We're asking nicely. The least you can do is answer the question."

"You seem to somehow forget that you are not the one in charge here, Englishman," Chaplin said condescendingly.

Hawk stared at Ilse. "Can I do it now please?"

There was a look of resignation on her face. "Charge, Jake."

Hawk moved swiftly. His right arm came up and bent at the elbow before he swung it out to the side, driving forcefully into the neck of the man standing next to him. The Frenchman instantly buckled at his knees as he started losing consciousness. While the man was going down, Hawk concentrated on the one to his left. This time his right arm came around, his large ham-like fist crashing against the surprised guard's jaw.

Still in motion, the former SAS man reached down and ripped the handrail from the top of the carriage seat. He swung it like a baseball bat at the head of the third French guard. It connected solidly and with a vibrating ring, caved in the man's jaw, blood spattering across the carriage window.

This left one more guard and Chaplin still standing. The guard had his handgun lifted and pointed in Hawk's direction. He reached out, grabbing the weapon, twisting savagely. The gun fired as the man's finger broke in the trigger guard. The bullet passed close to Hawk's ear. The Talon operator ignored it, instead turning the weapon on the shooter, slipping his own finger through the guard and firing.

The man's head snapped back as a bullet punched into it, just above his bridge of his nose. Blood and brain splattered back through the carriage, part of it spraying Chaplin's face.

The kidnap specialist now had his own gun moving towards Hawk. However, the former SAS man was also still in motion, and by the time the Frenchman's weapon snapped into line, Hawk's was pointing straight at his head. He smiled. "Well, Charlie, I do believe we've got ourselves a stalemate."

"I believe so, my English friend."

"Just so you understand it, I'm not your friend."

Ilse shook her head in wonderment. "Shit, Jake, where did that come from?"

He winked at her. "Kind of a hidden talent that I have."

One of the men on the floor beside Hawk moaned. The former SAS man looked down, recognizing who it was. He lifted his boot and brought it down hard on the man's arm. The man screamed with pain as the bones in it broke clean through. "Told you I was going to break your arm." Then he kicked him in the side of the head, knocking him out.

"What now?" Chaplin asked.

Ilse said, "The offer still stands."

He looked at his men, scattered on the floor of the carriage. "It would seem that I have but little choice."

Hawk said, "Lower your gun and we'll talk."

Chaplin followed the order, and the former SAS man did the same. "Where would you like me to start?"

"The beginning is always a good place."

The Frenchman sighed. "A few weeks back I was approached by a man for a job. He brought me photos and a name."

"Do you know who he was? His name?" Ilse asked.

"In this business, you're better off not knowing names."

"What did he look like?" Hawk asked.

"He looked just like you and me. Average height, average build."

"You say just like you and me, what nationality?"

"I think he was Swiss."

Hawk looked at Ilse. She said, "Makes sense, Switzerland does some trade with North Korea."

Chaplin raised his eyebrows. "Wait a minute. Did you say North Korea?"

"That's right," Hawk said. "North Korea. Section Three to be more precise."

The Frenchman shook his head. "I never did any deal with North Koreans. I told you he was Swiss."

"Yeah, more than likely a fucking middleman, you stupid twat."

"Tell me what happened with the girl," Ilse said.

"We did our reconnaissance and then we set up the pickup. It was quite easy actually. She was out at a night-club. She had a few too many drinks; left on her own. We just drove up beside her with a van, put her in and took her away."

"When did you make delivery?"

"The next morning. We don't hold onto them too long. There's too much can happen," Chaplain explained. "Even when we sedate them."

Hawk wanted to punch the man in the face. "Where did the exchange take place?"

"Here, of course. There's not many people getting around an old disused rail yard."

"Is there anything about the Swiss man that stood out?" Hawk asked.

Chaplin thought for a moment. "He spoke like a well-educated man, wore an expensive suit, had a Rolex watch."

"Sounds like a banker to me."

"Why would you say that?" asked Ilse. "Not all Swiss gentlemen are bankers."

"He's rich, he's well dressed, and he's in a position to meet lots of people. Hell, I know at least two Swiss bankers that were booking agents for assassins."

"Booking agents?"

"You know what I mean."

"I suppose it would give him the opportunity to meet people from the North Korean side of things."

Hawk looked at Chaplin. "Did he seem nervous to you at all?"

The Frenchman shook his head. "No, he was actually quite calm."

"So he's done this before then. I thought maybe he might have been coerced in some way. But it looks as though he wasn't. We need to find him."

Ilse cocked her head towards Chaplin. "What about him?"

"You said you were going to let me go," Chaplin pointed out.

"Then you better get out of here before I change my mind," Hawk warned him.

Chaplin disappeared from the carriage. Ilse said, "You're going to let him go just like that?"

"I have a feeling he won't get far."

She looked at the fallen men in the carriage. "That was something else."

"You should see me when I'm angry. I turn green."

Without warning, loud voices emanated from just outside the carriage. They glanced at each other before moving to the shattered windows of the carriage to look out. Four figures had a fifth pinned to the ground and were flexi cuffing his hands behind his back. Grizz Harvey looked up and said, "You two all right?"

"I'd kill for a beer." He grinned at their rescuers.

"What is going on?" Chaplin called out. "You let me go free."

"I did. I kept my word. They didn't give theirs though."

The Frenchman let out a long string of curses directed at the Englishman. Nemo Kent clipped him behind the ear and said, "Shut the fuck up or I'll gag you."

"You get anything, Jake?" Harvey asked.

"I think we might have."

CHAPTER EIGHTEEN

Zurich, Switzerland

ANJA LOOKED at her people gathered around the table. She placed the folder in front of them and then flicked it open. "Take a sheet, study it. It will tell you what you need to know about your target."

Hawk picked the paper up then saw a photo beneath it in the folder. Looking at Anja, he pointed at the picture then grasped it and waved it at her. "What is this place?"

"Bank der Welt," Anja said. "Or Bank of the World. Thirty floors of financial center. Our target has an office on the top floor."

"It's always the top floor," Hawk moaned.

"As you can see by the information you have in front of you, Karl was able to get us a name. Silvan Bauer. He's an international banker amongst other things."

"What other things?" Hawk asked.

"He is a broker who makes connections between certain types of people."

"Bloody assassins."

"Among other things, yes. When Karl dug deeper, he came up with a link to a man named Kim Chang-Ho. He's a North Korean businessman. However, if you look below the surface of his profile he has links to North Korean intelligence."

"So do you think he could be the head of Section Three?" Ilse asked.

"In Europe it could be a possibility. The thing is, we don't know where to find him. Which is why we need our friend Bauer. We question Bauer, we find Kim."

Hawk frowned. "I don't see a picture of Kim there."

"That's because no one really knows what he looks like."

"You're shitting me."

"No, Mr. Hawk, I am not shitting you."

"Wow. You're telling me that for all the intelligence communities there are across Europe no one can come up with a known likeness of this guy? What about the Yanks?"

"No one."

"So I'm guessing we really need to take this guy alive?"

Anja bobbed her head. "You guessed right."

"So what is the plan?"

"Being what it is, security is thick on the ground," Anja explained. "First, we need to set off the alarms to create some confusion. That'll give you approximately 5 to 10 minutes to get up to the top floor and isolate the target. Normally, when the fire alarms go off, the lifts stop moving. Karl will be able to isolate them. You'll be able to use them. We also need to isolate the security camera feed."

"Sounds like a plan," Hawk greed.

"Just to make it seem real, one of Mr. Harvey's men will set off a smoke bomb on the 5th floor. Jake, it'll be you and Ilse who will go to the top floor to question our friend. Once you get in the elevator, you'll need to put masks on. I don't want anybody able to identify you. You'll be armed, so the confusion should help the suspicion to be drawn away from you. Are there any questions?"

"When do we go?"

Anja looked at her watch. "In thirty minutes. Question him onsite. Do not attempt to get him out."

"What about his bodyguards?"

"Use your discretion."

"Copy that."

"That is all. Good luck."

Anja held Hawk back. "Mr. Hawk, this man is a danger to society. In my opinion, he can't be allowed to walk away free. And you can't get him out of there. So..."

"I can join the dots. I'll take care of it. There probably will be a problem though."

"Ilse?"

"Yes, she's good at everything she does, but she's not quite conditioned for this."

Anja nodded. "I understand what you mean. She's a very good Intel officer and also quite a capable field officer. But to be able to do what we do, she's going to have to take the next step."

"Yes, ma'am."

———

"IS EVERYONE IN POSITION?"

They called in one at a time, confirming that they were. Nemo Kent had already made his way inside, posing as an electronics repairman. Outside in the van with the rest of Harvey's team were Hawk and Ilse. Both were dressed in long coats to hide their weapons underneath. Harvey, Linc, and MacBride were to act as backup should things go wrong and get out of hand.

Anja and Karl were both watching from the safety of their crib. "All right, people. Let's do this."

Hawk and Ilse climbed out of the van and started

across the street to the building's broad glass front. At its center were two large sliding doors. As they approached, Karl hit a single button and the alarms started going crazy.

Both security guards on the outside were startled and turned to run inside. Both were armed with MP5s.

Hawk and Ilse followed them in through the doors. The alarms inside were loud, causing people to start to panic. Everybody was so concerned with looking after their own safety, they didn't notice the two people walking the opposite direction. The former SAS operator said in a low voice, "Pop smoke, Nemo."

"Roger that."

The two of them walked towards the bank of elevators in the far corner. Hawk pressed the button and waited patiently for the car to arrive. "What's happening, Karl?"

"Just moving to the next phase, Jake."

On the other end of the comms Karl was already putting it in motion. He made a call and waited for the answer. "Yes, my name is Fabian. I'm from your alarm monitoring service. Listen, our board is going crazy over here. I'm just letting you know that it's a false alarm. No need for anything urgent."

He listened for a moment. "Yes, inform Mr. Bauer. We're very sorry."

Karl disconnected the call and then said, "OK, target is remaining in his office. He's yours for the taking."

In the elevator, both Hawk and Ilse put on their ski masks. They then took out the two pump action shotguns from beneath their long coats. Hawk jacked in a round and said, "Are you ready?"

"Yes."

"Follow my lead."

The elevator stopped and the door slid open. As soon as Hawk stepped out, there were cries of alarm. He turned to his left and started walking around a large counter, which served as a reception area for the top floor. Immediately, the receptionist, a woman with long black hair, slipped beneath the desk, taking a phone with her. Hawk knew it would do her no good because all communications were now jammed.

A man in a suit stood at a junction of the open walkway. He fumbled with his coat to get his handgun free from its holster. Hawk lifted the shotgun and fired.

The security guard grunted, doubled over from the solid blow of the beanbag round, incapacitated as he sank to his knees; lay on his side. The former SAS man jacked another round into the breech and just then another man appeared at the end of the walkway. To Hawk's right and slightly behind him, the shotgun that Ilse held roared to life.

Another beanbag round exploded from the weapon's muzzle. It hit the man flush in his chest, punching him back against the wall, so he was pinned there for a moment before sliding down.

They were effective without the risk of innocent casualties.

Suddenly, the evacuation of the top floor moved like a flood. Hawk turned the corner and before him stood a large glass cube. On the inside were three men, one behind a desk while two others stood talking to him. As soon as they saw the former SAS man, they reached inside their coats, each pulling out a handgun. Hawk let the shotgun hang by its strap before pulling his own weapon from within his long coat.

The SIG came up and roared twice. The front wall of the glass cube shattered, and little brick-like shards of safety glass fell like confetti at a wedding. One of Bauer's bodyguards opened fire and Hawk felt the passage of the two rounds as they fizzed past.

The former SAS man pointed his SIG center mass of the man that had fired at him and squeezed the trigger.

The man dropped to the carpeted floor, blood starting to pool the moment he found it.

Beside him, Ilse fired her own weapon. Three bullets hammered into the second guard and his arms windmilled as he was punched backwards. He fell over a chair, which tipped with him under his weight. The wood splintered and he lay still.

Hawk and Ilse stepped inside the office. Hawk spoke, his SIG pointed at the man's face, "I figure you've got two minutes to live, if you don't answer our questions. If you do, you might even come out of this alive."

"What do you want?"

"You're a go between for Section Three." It was a statement, not a question. "A few weeks ago, you hired a man to do a job for you. That job had a name. Polly White. I want to know where she is."

Bauer shook his head. "I don't—"

BLAM!

The bullet from the SIG punched into his left shoulder, causing him to cry out in pain. "Not the right fucking answer. Try again."

"Wait, wait."

"Come on, Bauer, Kim Chang-Ho. Did he take delivery of the girl?"

Hawk saw the flicker in his eyes and that told him all he needed to know. "What did he want her for? Speak up, we've only got a couple of minutes left."

"It was something to do with a list."

"Did he say what list?" asked Hawk already knowing the answer.

"No."

"Where was he taking her?"

"I don't know."

"Try again."

"Honest, I don't know."

"Where have they set up? Where do they have their base of operations?" Ilse asked.

"Zeeland. The flooded zone."

"The flooded zone?"

"There is an island in the middle. That is where they are."

Hawk stared at him and nodded. "I think I believe you."

He was about to pull the trigger when Ilse beat him to it. Bauer's head snapped back, and he died with a surprised expression on his face.

The Talon operator looked at her. "Bloody hell."

"We couldn't leave him alive. Now we need to go."

"Yes, we do."

"WHAT DID WE LEARN?" Anja asked.

"Section Three have set up shop in the Zeeland Flooded Zone," Ilse said.

The flood zone dated back to World War Two. The Germans had flooded great portions of the area as they had fallen back under the pressure of Canadians driving them further north. Whole villages and towns went underwater until after the war, when areas were drained. Except for one portion that was left underwater. At the center of this large flat plain was a small rise, on it a village. No one had gone back to it after the war.

"Karl, see if we've got a picture of the Zeeland Flooded Zone, please," Anja said. "While he's doing that, what else did we learn?"

Hawk shook his head. "Not a lot. Section Three call the place home; they've set up their base there. We don't even know if the girl is there. We'll need to run a recon to determine what we're facing. Possibly all hands on deck."

He looked at Grizz Harvey. The big man nodded. "Just say when and where, Jake; we'll be there."

"I have some pictures," Karl said. A couple flashed up on the screen. One was like a lake with buildings sticking out of it. The other was an island with even more of the same, though these were high and dry "The first picture you see is one of houses that flooded when the Nazis blew holes in dikes. The second is the small village, the only village that is high and dry out of the water. According to what you're saying, Jake, this is where Section Three is holed up."

"How far away are those houses from the village?"

"I don't know, it's just a picture. I'll need to look at satellite images and maps to figure that out."

"How long before you can have an Intel package?"

"I'll get started on one right away."

"Thanks, Karl."

"It looks like a lot of open ground, or should I say water, Jake," Anja pointed out. "Do you think you can get to the village undetected?"

"We'll have to use the dark, but yeah, I think we can do it. What do you think, Grizz?"

"If we can get a building close enough to the island. Set Nemo up in it as overwatch, he can cover our approach."

"We could use one of those buildings if we can get one, like you say, close enough, as a forward observation point," Hawk said. "Insert during the night lay up during the day. Then the following night we go in. Karl, we need a good house."

"Don't worry, Jake. I'll find you one."

———

FIVE OF THEM sat around the table looking at the intel package that Karl and Ilse had put together. It was the latter who stabbed a finger at the map where she'd just placed a circle. "The houses are around five-hundred meters from the island. They would make a good launch point for you to infiltrate the camp. There is a two-floor house here. Can you work with that, Nemo?"

The operator looked at the picture. "I'll make it work, ma'am."

Hawk said, "It'll make a good OP to see if we can work out if our target is there."

Harvey nodded. "We'll lay up for the day and then if we can ascertain she's there, then we'll go after dark. If not, we'll disappear, and we can pass intel onto the right people."

"How are we inserting?" Hawk asked.

"On foot," Anja told him. "I assume you'll take a small inflatable with you for your equipment?"

Hawk nodded. "Most likely. Grizz?"

"Seems it would be best," Harvey agreed.

"Can you get us some claymores?" Hawk asked.

"Maybe."

"Cool. And maybe some C-4."

"You want me to get a MOAB, too?"

"No, might be a bit of overkill," he replied with a grin.

"Get me a list and I'll get what you need."

"Yes, ma'am."

"Is there anything else?"

Nemo cleared his throat.

Harvey winked at Hawk. "He's going to ask for a new toy."

"Mister Kent?" Anja asked.

"An Accuracy International AWM chambered for Three-Three-Eight, please, ma'am."

"Shit," Hawk groaned. "They're only going to be five-hundred meters away. Not in Germany."

"I told you." Harvey grinned.

"Bigger stopping power, ma'am, and if I have to shoot through walls, well..."

"Put it on the list."

"Thank you, ma'am."

"Gentlemen, you will be on your own. Other than a helo for extract, there will be no QRF to help you. You'll have to rely on each other."

Hawk gave a wry smile. "You're singing my song."

"You dig this shit?" Harvey asked.

"Only the dangerous stuff."

"You are seriously twisted, brother."

Hawk gave him a big grin. "Hold my beer."

"Shit."

CHAPTER NINETEEN

The Flooded Zone, Zeeland

THE TEAM MOVED through the water; Hawk out front on point where he felt at home. Out of the darkness around a hundred meters away loomed the gathering of rundown buildings which was their destination.

They had been inserted on dry land and started their journey on foot through the waist-deep water towards their objective. At the rear of the small column was Nemo, watching their six. In front of him, pulling the small rubber raft was Mac MacBride.

Hawk stopped as the moon came out from behind the clouds overhead giving a clearer picture of what lay before them. "Wait here."

Harvey and his men held up as Hawk kept moving forward. "Alpha Two, copy?"

"Copy, Bravo."

"I'm moving toward the OP. How are we looking?"

"Nothing on ISR, Jake."

"Copy, out."

He pressed forward until he reached the buildings, then moved in between them. Even in the darkness, he could tell that many were missing boards on their exterior, and the glass windowpanes were gone. Some structures were lucky to be standing at all.

When he reached the target building, he pushed the door open. In front of him was a set of stairs leading to the second floor, the wooden treads and risers rotting away from their constant immersion in water. He stepped up. Moving inside through the doorway.

Hawk swept the area using his night vision goggles to peer through the darkness. He moved to the stairs and proceeded slowly, each tentative step testing weight to be sure they would not collapse beneath him.

When he reached the landing, he went to his left, then opened the door almost opposite. Across to the window he looked towards the island where Section Three now had their camp set up in the village. The place was mostly blacked out, but you could still see the odd light every now and again.

Hawk said into his comms, "Bring them on in, Grizz."

Minutes later, the rest of the team was inside. They all made their way upstairs into the room where Hawk stood waiting. The former SAS man indicated the village over on the island. "There it is."

Harvey nodded. "You men get some rest. Nemo, you're first watch."

"Roger that," replied Nemo Kent as he settled down beside the window.

Hawk looked at Harvey. "Do you want to go and have a look?"

The big operator raised his eyebrows. "You mean right now?"

"Shit, yeah. No time like the present."

"Just you and me?"

"Can't take Anja, can we?"

"Let's do it."

They checked their weapons. Both were armed with

suppressed Bren2s. Harvey said to Nemo, "You just graduated to overwatch."

"You pair are fucking crazy."

"He's the crazy one," Harvey replied. "I'm just going along to make sure he stays out of trouble."

"Yeah, but who's going to keep you out of trouble?" he muttered.

———

THEY CAME out of the water and dropped to the ground as an armed guard passed by. Allowing a further 30 seconds to elapse, they came to their feet and hurried across to one of the buildings close by.

The pair pressed their backs against the wall and waited. The last thing they needed right then was to be seen. Hawk slid along the side of the building and around its rear. From there, he made his way towards the center of the village, keeping to the shadows. They counted at least eight guards wandering about the place.

At the center of the village was a larger building which butted up to a tiny square. Two men stood out front and Hawk guessed that this was their HQ. He looked up onto the roof top and saw a large aerial reaching towards the sky. He whispered to Harvey, "HQ and communications center."

"It's got me how they've lasted out here without anyone knowing," the big man said.

"Money will buy you a lot of things. Including privacy."

They remained in place for a further five minutes before moving on, narrowly avoiding another roving patrol before stopping near another building. "Where do you figure she is? If they've got her?" Harvey asked.

"I'd say she'll be close to the main building."

"I agree."

Hawk was about to say something but clamped his mouth shut as two more men walked past their position. "Let's get out of here."

———

"I THINK WE MIGHT HAVE SOMETHING," Linc said over their comms.

Hawk glanced at Harvey before coming to his feet. They both went upstairs into the room where the big operator was watching the small village. Beside him was an open Toughbook. "What's up?"

"ISR just picked up an X-ray taking food to one of the buildings."

"Sounds promising. Alpha Two, sitrep?"

"It looks like there could be a prisoner in that building, Jake. There are no guards but considering where they are, there's no real need."

"We'll make that our target."

"We also have an update on the possible number of X-rays onsite."

"Send."

"Twenty. Two Zero. Copy?"

"Copy, two zero. Out."

Hawk looked at Harvey. "Gather everybody around. It's time to go to work."

A few minutes later, every man was gathered around as they discussed the plan for that night. "How clear is your field of fire from here?" Hawk asked Nemo.

"It's not great, but it'll work."

"Fine. I'll go after the girl. Grizz, you and the others go after the prize. Chang-Ho. If he's anywhere, it'll be in that main building."

"That's only a two-person job, Jake," Harvey pointed out. "I'll have Linc set up the claymores."

"Fine by me. Once I get the girl I'll pull back. Nemo,

keep an eye out because I'm guessing you'll have to cover our retreat. This is not a scalpel raid, gentlemen. It's a fucking sledgehammer. Send them a message."

"Bravo, this is Alpha One, change channel."

Hawk glanced at Harvey who gave him a quizzical stare. The former SAS man raised his eyebrows. "Changing channel now, Boss."

He walked out of the room. "Go ahead."

"I'm bringing on Frank Fitzgerald, Jake. He has a pressing problem."

"I'm listening."

"Mister Hawk, there's been what you would call a substantial leak about your mission."

Hawk felt his ire start to rise. If there was something he hated it was loose lips. Especially when it endangered his life.

When he said nothing, Fitzgerald continued. "Word of your operation has been leaked to Section Three by White."

"What the fuck? What's his game?"

"I think it's all getting the better of him. We've been able to ascertain that he's still been in contact with the North Koreans through back channels. He's getting desperate in spite of what he's been saying. I'm afraid to say we think he's only one step away from giving over the list. Which is why I've sent people to pick him up."

"What are you going to do, Jake?" Anja asked.

"Have you been able to trace anything?"

"Yes, all communications point to Zeeland."

"Which means she's here. We'll continue mission. However, I'm going to need something from you."

"Name it."

"Get me a UAV before tonight."

"I don't think I can, Jake."

"I can," said Fitzgerald. "Leave it with me. What do you want?"

"Don't care as long as it's fully loaded."

"It will be."

"I'll let the others know."

He signed off and went back into the room with Harvey and the others. "I am the bearer of bad news," he informed them.

"Kinda figured that," Harvey replied.

Hawk went on to tell them what was happening. "I told them the mission is still a go."

"As you should," grunted Harvey. He looked at his men. "Volunteers only."

"Fuck off," Linc shot back at him.

He looked at the others. "Looks like we're all in, Jake."

The Brit grinned. "Tally ho."

"THREE...TWO...ONE...EXECUTE."

The Bren kicked back against Hawk's shoulder and the guard near the door dropped. Meanwhile across the compound, Harvey and Mac MacBride did the same. Only two of their targets dropped. "X-ray down," Hawk said.

"Confirm," Harvey replied.

Hawk crossed the open area and stopped near the dead guard. "Entering the target building."

"Copy. Eagle Team is breaching."

"Hold! Hold! Hold!"

Hawk froze and dropped to a knee when Ilse's voice crackled across the comms. "What's going on?"

"I have a group of X-rays to the north sweeping in your direction. Thirty to forty in number."

"How the hell did they get that many on site without us noticing. Shit. Grizz, fall back on my position."

"Roger, Jake. We're moving."

"Linc, sitrep?"

"Just placing the last few. Five minutes."

"Nemo, any movement?"

"I've got some, Jake," the sniper confirmed.

"Make it rain."

"Sending."

There was only one thing left for Hawk to do. He breached.

———

THE SOUND of gunfire shattered the night, especially inside the confines of the small room. However, Hawk had thrown a flashbang before he went in and the shooter on the inside had sprayed weapon fire everywhere like a lunatic. Two well-placed rounds from the Bren put him down.

Hawk swept the room and found it empty. "Shit, no joy, I say again, no joy. Alpha Two I need a sweep of this entire place to see if the package is still in play."

"You need to get out, Jake, there's X-rays all over the place."

"Just find me something, Ilse. I'll take even the smallest thing you can give me."

"Shit. Wait one, Jake."

"I'm not going anywhere."

———

Antwerp, Belgium

"Karl, I want everything you can see on that big screen now," Ilse demanded.

She stood there, hands on hips, staring at the darkened screen that had figures running across it. "Zoom out."

The screen adjusted so it encompassed every building. Figures were moving left and right, running around like little ants. Her eyes kept scanning the screen looking for something, anything that would give cause to suspect Polly White's presence. "Come on, where are you?"

"What is going on, Ilse?" Anja asked.

"I'm trying to find anything that might indicate where Polly White is being held."

"Forget it, order Jake and the team out."

"I already did that. He's not going."

"Bravo, this is One, over."

"Have you found me something yet?"

"Negative. You need to get your ass out of there."

"Not until you find me that target, ma'am," came the stubborn reply.

"Damn it, Jake."

"Keep looking, we're wasting time."

Ilse heard her hiss something under her breath but never took her eyes off the screen. Anja stared at what she was looking at and said, "How does he expect us to find something in that?"

Ilse's eyes darted left and right, up and down. Then, "I have something."

"Where?"

"Second building from the left, two down. Everybody is running around moving on the position where our men are. Except for that one."

"You're right. That has to be her. She's locked inside."

"Jake, do you copy?"

"I'm still here."

"Northeast side of the village. I'll guide you in. She's inside one of the buildings."

"Roger that. Moving now."

———

A shooter loomed up out of the darkness and Hawk's suppressed Bren2 put him down with two rounds into the chest. He moved forward into the shadows of another building and paused. "Grizz, where are you?"

"Headed back in your direction," came the reply.

"I'm going to circle around. We've got a line on the package. Draw them in on you and spring the trap."

"Roger that. Good luck."

Hawk pushed to the east.

"Jake, X-rays coming your way."

He stopped once more and pressed his back against the wood of the building he was beside. Two men appeared and he stepped out, cutting them down with a savage burst. As he pressed forward, Hawk dropped out the magazine in the Bren and made a tactical reload, replacing it with a fresh one.

"Jake, turn right and go straight on. The way is clear for the moment."

"Copy," he replied in a low voice.

Across the isolated village rooftops, the sound of gunfire peaked violently and was followed by a series of blasts which made the earth tremble beneath the Talon operator's feet. He flicked his NVGs up just in time to see the fireballs rise into the darkened sky. Linc had detonated the claymores.

THE EXPLOSIONS SEEMED to swallow the advancing North Korean shooters like a hungry beast devouring everything in its path. The sound waves rolled across the flat waters of the flooded zone leaving behind the screams of the wounded, and burning buildings.

Harvey glanced at Linc. "What the hell did you do?"

"I might have brought a little extra bang along."

"Shit." He said into his comms, "Alpha Two this is Eagle One, over."

"Copy, Eagle One."

"Need an update, over."

"Grizz, you've got another group of X-rays pushing down towards you from the north. Jake is moving to the target."

"Copy." He turned to Linc. "Flank right, let's go."

They worked their way around one of the partially destroyed buildings which was still burning. "How much shit did you use?" Mac asked.

"Little bit."

"Fuck."

"Eagle One, they're almost in position," Ilse said over the comms.

Harvey suddenly changed direction between two buildings. His Bren2 came up level as he pressed forward towards the new threat. Emerging from the alley, Harvey started firing. Deliberate, methodical. He was soon joined by the other two men with him, and their weapons joined the party.

The gunmen from Section 3 were knocked down indiscriminately in the crossfire not realizing they'd been in immediate danger.

The firing stopped and Harvey scanned the area through the green of his NVGs. "All right, pull back to the water. We'll make a stand there."

"Roger that."

"Jake, we're pulling back to Point Zulu. We'll hold there for you."

"Copy. If you have to leave, don't wait."

"We'll see. Out."

"JAKE, COMING UP ON YOUR RIGHT."

Hawk turned, sighted, fired. Switched his aim, and repeated. Two more X-rays down. But at least he was almost at his destination. As he crossed the last bit of open ground, he let the Bren hang by its strap and drew his SIG.

The Brit swept to his left and right before climbing the three steps onto the broken-down stoop.

Keeping the gun level in his right hand, Hawk pushed the door open with his left and stepped into the gloom. His flashlight came on and he flicked it around the room.

Polly White was huddled in the corner, pressing herself further back at the perceived threat. Hawk said, "I'm a friend."

"You're British?" There was surprise in her voice.

"Are you Polly White?"

"Yes."

"Alpha Two, jackpot. I say again, jackpot."

"Alpha Two copies."

Hawk started forward. "I'm here to get you out."

"Did my father send you?" she asked.

"Something like that. Can you—"

The crash of the gunshot caused Polly White to cry out. The hammer blow hit Hawk square in the back and thrust him forward. He staggered and fell to his knees before falling to the floor, dropping the flashlight.

The dark shadow stepped inside and grunted with satisfaction. "That is one that will not see the sun tomorrow."

Polly started to sob.

"Shut your whore mouth," the man snarled. "I should kill you now, but your father has agreed to give us the list for your release."

"No," she gasped. "He wouldn't dare."

"Never underestimate the power of blood," the man said.

He walked closer to the crouching girl, stepping over Hawk's prone form. He stood over her and sneered. "Soon your ordeal will be over and we shall be rid of both you and your father."

It took a moment to realize what the North Korean was saying. "No, you can't just kill me."

"Just watch me."

Unaware of the movement behind him, the North Korean stepped forward. Another weapon fired, this one quieter than the shot the North Korean fired. However, the shooter never stopped at one shot, there were four of them. The North Korean fell forward with a grunt of pain.

Hawk climbed to his feet, slowly, painfully. "Good thing I had my rear plate in, dickhead."

"Are you all right?"

"I'll live," he said, picking up his flashlight and shone it on the dead North Korean. It was Chang-Ho. "Come on, we're getting out of here."

He helped her to her feet. "Follow me and stay close."

Hawk led her out the door. As he paused to look around, making sure the way was clear, Polly asked, "Was what he said true? Did my father agree to give him what he wanted?"

He ignored the question. "Bravo One to all call signs, I have the package, moving to extract."

"Copy, Jake," Harvey replied. "Nemo, close on us."

"On my way."

Hawk said, "Alpha Two, that helo better be there."

"Airborne as we speak, Jake. You've got five minutes to get to the LZ."

"Why do I sense there's a but?"

"There are a good number of hostiles between you and the LZ, Jake. They've just started closing on your position."

Already? He thought for a moment. "Shit. Did they inject you with anything when they picked you up?"

"What?"

"I don't have time for this. Alpha Three can you try to scan for low frequency waves?"

"Wait one, Jake."

"I don't have fucking time to wait one."

"Language over the comms network, Bravo One," Anja reminded him.

"I can say it in fucking German, too."

"Breathe, Jake," Ilse said in a calm voice. "We'll get you both out of there."

The next voice was Karl's. "You're right Jake, there is a low frequency transmission coming from somewhere close. My guess is that she has a tracker embedded somewhere and if she moves outside of that building where she was it sets off a silent alarm which all of them pick up."

"Christ, we're only on the stoop."

"I don't know, Jake."

"Wait here," he snapped at Polly before walking out onto the village street. He looked around and saw something that might help their situation.

"Jake if you're going to do something, now is the time," Ilse said.

"Pick up Grizz first then have the pilot look for the largest building in the village. He'll find us there."

"What are you going to do, Jake?" Anja asked.

"Hopefully something that works."

"Shit."

"Language over comms—"

"Shut up, Jake. Just get yourself out of there alive."

"Yes, ma'am."

He hurried across to where Polly White waited nervously. "Come with me."

They rushed out onto the street and no sooner had they done, gunfire ripped along the rugged thoroughfare. "Down!" Hawk shouted as he turned and opened fire at the figures that had suddenly appeared behind them.

One fell but more appeared to take the fallen one's place. Then on the left more shooters opened fire and soon Hawk was under intense incoming rounds. He dropped flat.

"Mother—"

BOOM! An explosion close told him they had grenades.

"Viper One-One, this is Bravo, over."

"Read you Bravo," came the voice in his comms.

"I need a fire mission right now. Danger close, over."

"Roger, Bravo. Ahh—I'm going to need clearance—"

"Danger close, Viper, send it!"

"Roger. Keep your head down, Bravo. Good luck."

"Will mark position."

Hawk reached and turned on the strobe fixed to his shoulder.

"Got you, Bravo."

"Target is north and east of my position."

"On its way."

Hawk slid over and lay atop Polly White while bullets kicked up debris all around them. "Keep your head down, girl, this is going to be bonkers."

Suddenly the world seemed to be ripped apart as not one, but two AGM-114 Hellfire missiles crashed earthward and exploded violently.

Bodies were flung skyward along with earth and rock as the North Korean shooters were decimated by the airstrike engulfing them. Not waiting, Hawk dragged Polly to her feet. "Come on, girl."

They ran through the carnage, and the burning building nearby illuminated a scene of devastation of charred and limbless bodies. "Don't look."

Once beyond it, Hawk kept them both moving. In the distance he could hear gunfire and knew that would be Harvey and his men dealing in death. But mixed with the sharp cracks came another sound. The deep WHOP-

WHOP-WHOP of the approaching helo for their extraction.

Hawk and Polly reached the double-floored house with the gently pitched rooftop. He reached into his pocket and pulled out his flashlight. "Take this and get up to the second floor."

"What are you going to do?"

"Somebody has to stay behind."

"What? You're not serious?" she gasped.

"Figure of speech, darling. Now, get up there."

She disappeared inside, the flashlight beam bouncing over the floor and walls as she went.

"Alpha Two, copy?"

"I'm here, Bravo."

"Sitrep."

"We can see you, Jake. You've still got more X-rays closing in on your position."

"How the hell did they all get here?" he wondered out loud.

"Question for another day," came the reply. "The helicopter is currently extracting Eagle Team—"

"Man down! Man down!"

The call broke through the transmission and Hawk's blood ran cold. It wasn't Harvey because it was his voice he was hearing.

"Eagle Team has a man down hard."

"Confirm, Eagle One," Anja responded. "What's his status?"

"Eagle is priority four, over."

"Confirm priority four."

Hawk was stunned for a moment. One of Harvey's team was KIA. He shook it off. There would be time for grief later. They still had a mission to finish.

Bullets hammered the wood building behind Hawk, bringing him back to the present. He brought the Bren up and squeezed the trigger, forcing the two shooters who had appeared to take cover.

The Brit backed in through the open doorway and took cover behind the thin jamb. "Lot of good this'll do, Jake," he admonished himself.

He leaned around and fired another burst until the weapon emptied the magazine. He ducked back and dropped out the mag and replaced it with his last one. "Alpha Two, how long on that helo?"

"Still a few minutes, Jake."

"Copy."

He racked the charging handle and said, "I need a real-time update, Ilse."

"You have possibly ten X-rays closing on your position, Jake."

"Copy."

Bullets hit the front of the building and punched through the thin walls. Hawk leaned around the jamb once more and through his NVGs saw a shooter halfway through changing position. The Brit fired twice, single shots. The first plowed into the ground behind the running figure, the second knocked his right leg from beneath him and he went down in a tangle of arms and legs.

This brought forth a heavy fusillade of fire that seemed as though it would tear the front of the building off with wood splintering and rounds bursting through.

"Fuck me!" Hawk growled as he turned his back to the incoming fire.

He waited until the incoming storm eased a touch before reaching for one of the fragmentation grenades on his webbing. He pulled the pin, paused, then threw it.

The roar of the explosion was his cue to head for the stairs which he did, taking them two at a time. At the top on the landing, he turned right along the hallway. "Polly?"

"Here." She stepped out of a room. She looked more afraid now that what she had been when he found her.

"Don't worry, girl, we'll be fine. The helo is on its way. We just need to get to the roof."

He took the flashlight from Polly and looked at the ceiling. He found what he wanted and turned to her. "See that hatch up there? You're going up."

"I am?" She sounded surprised as he gave her the flashlight.

He picked her up effortlessly, boosting her high enough so she could reach out to the trap. "Push it open."

Polly reached up and the hatch moved. She pushed it across and once it was moved Hawk said, "Now pull yourself up."

She put the flashlight in her mouth and using every ounce of strength she had, dragged herself up through the opening.

"Do you see a ladder up there?"

The light flickered. "Yes."

Voices echoed up from the floor below. Hawk looked up. "Get the ladder down, I'll be back in a minute. If I don't come back, bash a hole through the roof. It's tile. Then climb out and wave the flashlight around so the helicopter can see you."

"Where are you going?"

"Just do it. Don't ask questions."

He went back to the landing and saw the men coming fast up the stairs. Hawk fired a long burst from the Bren until the magazine ran dry. He then let the weapon go, so it hung by its strap before pulling the SIG from its holster. He fired three fast rounds at the remaining man, who was still coming up, his weapon blazing fire. The ascending man staggered and fell backwards across the bodies of his fallen comrades.

Hawk grabbed the last of the fragmentation grenades from his webbing. He pulled the pin and then tossed it down to the foot of the stairs, just as more men entered through the open door.

The Brit dropped to the floor as the grenade exploded violently, shards of hot metal scything through the air, opening horrific wounds in the intruders.

Hawk quickly scrambled to his feet and ran back along the hallway. Polly had the ladder down and he tried his foot on the first rung. It held his weight, so he started to climb.

"Alpha Two, how far away is that helicopter?"

"One mike, Jake."

"Tell him we'll be on the roof."

"Roger that."

Once in the crawl space, Hawk went to work on the roof tiles. Within minutes he'd made a hole large enough for them to get through. He moved aside and said, "Climb up, quick."

Polly did as he said and climbed out the opening. He followed her through and onto the roof.

Looking around he could see the helicopter approaching. He searched his mind for the call sign. "Baker Two-One this is Bravo, over."

"Read you Lima Charlie, Bravo."

"I'm going to wave a flashlight around. We're on top of the only tall building in the village." Hawk paused. "Give me the flashlight, girl."

Polly passed it to Hawk, and he waved it towards the approaching Chinook. "I've got you, Bravo. We'll have you aboard British Airways in no time at all."

The Chinook came in, started to hover, then turned rear on to the building in an aerial dance. The rotor wash cascaded down in waves, battering the two below. Hawk wrapped his arms around Polly White to hold her steady.

While he did this the ramp on the Chinook was already lowering. Within moments it was only centimeters off the tiles. A voice came through Hawk's comms. "Ready when you are, Bravo."

Still being buffeted by the downdraft, Hawk helped Polly to her feet and the pair made their way onto the helicopter. No sooner were they aboard when the pilot had the bird moving up and away from the house.

Hawk sat Polly down and said, "Are you alright?"

She nodded.

Hawk looked around the inside of the dimly lit helicopter. He saw Harvey sitting next to the body bag on the floor. The big operator looked over at him.

"Who?" Hawk asked.

"Mac."

Hawk nodded. "I'm sorry, brother."

"Comes with the job. Is the girl alright?"

"Yeah."

"That's all that matters."

Yeah, that's all that matters.

EPILOGUE

Hereford, England, One Week Later

THEY BURIED Mac MacBride in England. It wasn't much of a burial, just the team, Mary Thurston, and Hank Jones. Hawk had eventually gotten around to asking Harvey what had happened.

"He was covering our six as we embarked. Last man. He was about to come up the ramp when he got hit. Nothing we could have done."

"He got any family?"

Harvey had shaken his head. "Nope."

The Brit left it at that.

Harvey and his two remaining men had gone out and got drunk that night. Hawk had left them to it. Although they were all a team, Harvey and his men were different. They'd been together a long time.

At the debriefing he ran through his part of the mission and confirmed that Chang-Ho was dead.

The following day brought more news. Damyan Dragov had been captured by Interpol and was locked away inside a secure facility. George White was also under lock and key as a guest of Her Majesty's Government.

Also, the remaining members of Section 3 had been mopped up by the Netherlands Armed Forces.

"Overall, not a bad result," Anja said to Hawk.

"But not good," Hawk pointed out.

She nodded.

Ilse said, "We still did some good, Jake. We saved Polly White."

"Yeah, but not the other one."

"You know we can't save them all, Jake. No matter how hard we try. We still have the satisfaction of knowing that Victor Medvedev is dead."

"That maybe so, but what kind of monster has replaced him?"

"That remains to be seen," Anja replied.

"Any word on a replacement for Mac?" Hawk asked.

"I'll go over that with Mister Harvey in a couple of days. I have looked over a few candidates. I would like his input though."

"Fucking shitty way to start a war," Hawk growled. "We've lost two people already."

Anja stared unblinkingly at him. "And we're bound to lose more, Jake. It's a sad truth about what we are trying to do. Tomorrow it could be me, Ilse, or even you. We've been lucky so far."

Hawk considered her words. "Yeah."

Karl appeared; he had a worried expression on his face. "We have just had a package delivered. You're going to want to take a look at this."

They got to their feet and followed him out into a recreation lounge. On the table was a box. Standing beside it was a delivery man. His face was etched with concern, bordering on fear. "I didn't do anything. I just delivered the package."

Hawk frowned but then he saw what was so concerning. The box had dark stains all around it. He stepped forward, taking a knife from his pocket.

"Be careful, Jake," Anja cautioned him.

He stepped closer to the box and stared at it. There were no postage marks on it anywhere. He looked at the delivery guy. "Where'd you get it?"

"Soho in London. The guy paid me five thousand pounds to bring it out here."

"And you didn't think that was kind of dodgy?" Hawk asked. "You have got to be having a laugh."

"It was five thousand pounds," the man whined in defense.

"Dickhead."

Hawk cut the tape on the box with his knife and peeled back the flaps. Inside was a plastic wrapped object with a note attached. Hawk picked up the stained paper, unfolded it and read the note.

A present from me to you. Ilya Noskov.

The Brit passed the piece of paper to Anja who read it then glanced worriedly at her operative. "Jake—"

"It's all right."

He started to fold back the plastic to reveal what was below the surface. Dark eyes stared back at him from the human head, the mouth wide in a silent scream. He looked over at Anja and said, "You can scratch Ansari off the list."

———

2 Days Later

"You are back," Leonid said as he watched Anja enter the room. "Tell me, how did things go?"

She stared at him. "Give me another name."

He held up a hand, the chain from the cuffs rattling on

242

the tabletop. "Wait, wait. I want something from you first. Did you get the girl?"

"Yes."

He stared at her. "Judging by the expression on your face I'd say it wasn't easy. I'd say you lost someone."

Anja shrugged her shoulders. The last thing she wanted to do is play games with this animal.

Leonid smiled expectantly. "It wasn't Jake, was it? Tell me it was him."

"No."

"But you did lose someone."

"So did Section Three."

"Oh, dear. They are very good at what they do. Which means you and your people are better. Maybe you are ready for this next one."

Anja leaned across the table, forcing the Russian to lean back. "Give me a fucking name," she growled savagely.

"Oh, you're going to love this one. Wolfgang Hermann."

"The German minister?"

Leonid's eyes lit up. "The one and only."

"But how?"

"By keeping it out of Germany. He hires people to do all of the work for him."

"Where?"

"Belgrade. That's where he peddles his specialty."

"And what does he specialize in?" Anja asked.

"African girls. He's like a modern-day slaver."

"Tell me more."

Leonid smiled. "You're going to have to go to Tanzania."

A LOOK AT BOOK THREE: TALON VENGEANCE

It all comes down to this...

Another name, another mission. This one in Tanzania. But it doesn't stay there. It spreads—and fast.

In the midst of mercenaries, dead lovers, and traitors abound, the Talon taskforce is made up of men and women nobody wanted. And their hard work is about to pay off in blood and bullets.

Two of their own will fall. One will survive. But at the end of the day...all that matters is that they stop Medusa. A task they mean to see right through to the stunning end.

Will this action-packed adventure ramp up to a victory against Medusa once and for all?

AVAILABLE JANUARY 2023

ABOUT THE AUTHOR

A relative newcomer to the world of writing, Brent Towns self-published his first book, a western, in 2015. *Last Stand in Sanctuary* took him two years to write. His first hardcover book, a Black Horse Western, was published the following year.

Since then, he has written 26 western stories, including some in collaboration with British western author, Ben Bridges.

Also, he has written the novelization to the upcoming 2019 movie from One-Eyed Horse Productions, titled, *Bill Tilghman and the Outlaws*. Not bad for an Australian author, he thinks.

Brent Towns has also scripted three Commando Comics with another two to come.

He says, "The obvious next step for me was to venture into the world of men's action/adventure/thriller stories. Thus, Team Reaper was born."

A country town in Queensland, Australia, is where Brent lives with his wife and son.

In the past, he worked as a seaweed factory worker, a knife-hand in an abattoir, mowed lawns and tidied gardens, worked in caravan parks, and worked in the hire industry. And now, as well as writing books, Brent is a home tutor for his son doing distance education.

Brent's love of reading used to take over his life, now it's writing that does that; often sitting up until the small hours, bashing away at his tortured keyboard where he loses himself in the world of fiction.

9 781685 491895